Fireball

NEW YORK *TIMES* BESTSELLING AUTHOR

ABBI GLINES

Visit my website at
www.abbiglinesbooks.com

Cover Designer: **Damonza.com**
Editor: Jovana Shirley, Unforeseen Editing
www.unforeseenediting.com
Formatting: Melissa Stevens, The Illustrated Author
www.theillustratedauthor.com

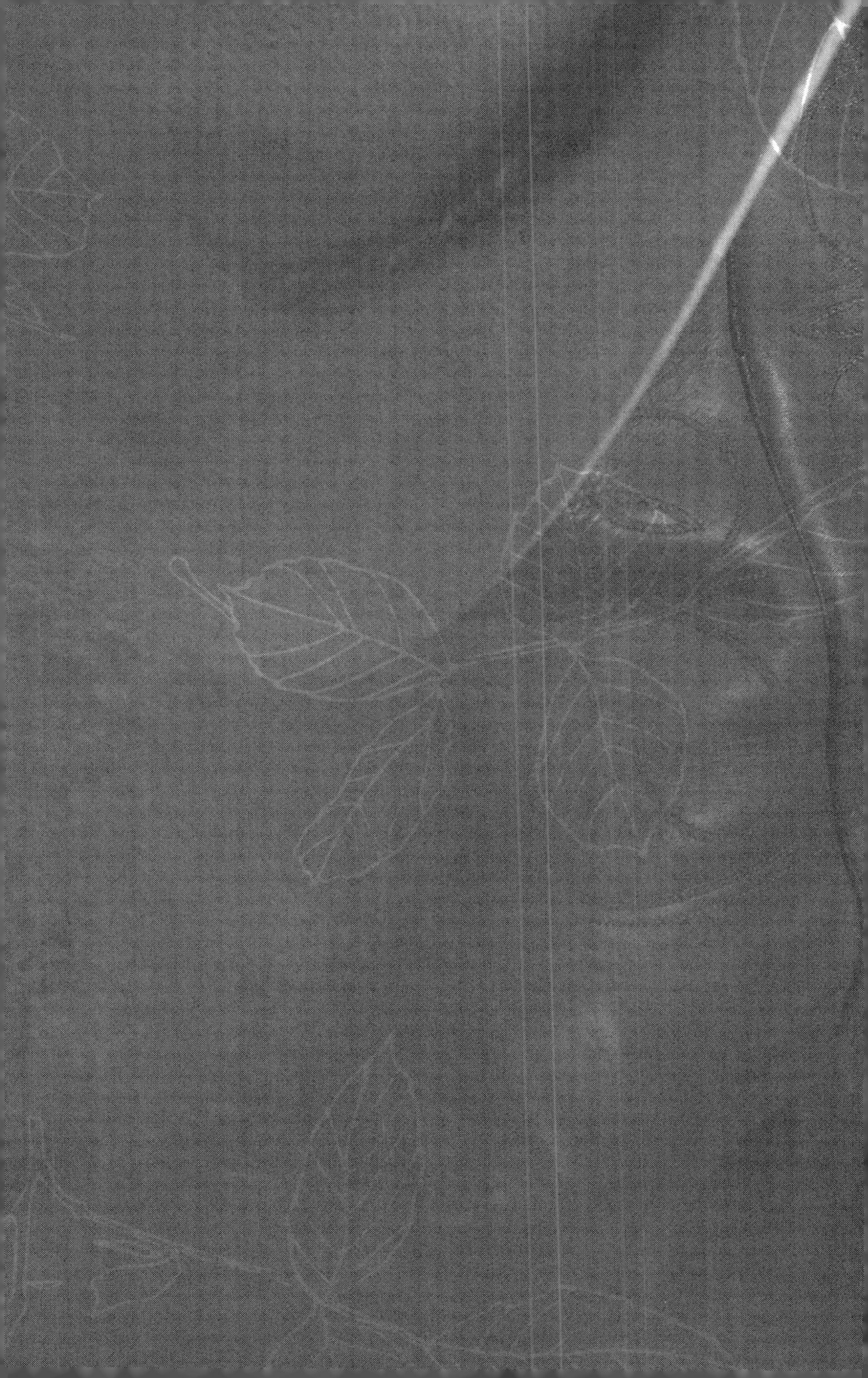

To Miriam Israel, the first baby I loved with my whole heart.
I was only five, but I was sure no one could ever take your place.
Sure, I always took the best Barbies and threatened to stop playing with you if I couldn't have the pink My Little Pony, but that's what big sisters are for.
We might be cousins, but in my heart, you'll always be my sister.

I

"Oh, what a tangled web we weave when first we practice to deceive."

—Sir Walter Scott

Chapter ONE

MADELINE

While outside on the balcony wrapped in a blanket with a cup of coffee in my hand, I stared off into the distance. The Smoky Mountains were chilly in the early morning, even in the summer. It was silent, except for the sounds of nature waking up. If I could find peace, this was the moment every day when I caught a glimpse of it. Before reality sank in.

Saxon was leaving today. He'd stayed with me for two weeks, but he needed to return to Moses Mile. I would miss his company even if I spoke very little. Just having someone here gave me a sense of security.

The Houstons wanted me to remain here, in their cabin, one they owned and rented out. Saxon's mother, Melanie, had said it gave her peace of mind. When I had fled, I'd had nowhere to go. There was no home for me anymore. After days of driving, unsure of where we were going, Saxon had brought me here.

There had been no calls or texts from Blaise in the almost three weeks since my world had been shattered. I should be relieved he was leaving me alone. Killing my father and brother was unforgivable. Explanations would never make it better. Nothing would.

But my heart had never felt so empty. I made it through each day, going through the motions. Knowing deep down that if he called, I'd answer. Just to hear his voice. I was ashamed of that.

The door behind me opened, and I didn't turn around to see Saxon. I knew he was leaving. I wasn't ready for that goodbye. He had helped the loneliness. A little. The fear of being alone was a part of me now. I would never be able to go back to the way I had once been.

"The fridge is stocked. You should be good for a week. I left a credit card on the counter. Use it. Mom wants to make sure you have all you need. She understands you don't feel like talking right now but wants you to call her when you do. She wants to visit you too."

He paused then, and I knew he wanted me to say that, yes, I'd call or that I wanted her to visit. But the truth was, Melanie wasn't someone I felt like I could rely on. She did what the Hughes said to do. After seeing the photos of my dad and Cole, I couldn't blame her.

"The rental car company will drop off your car today too," Saxon added when it was clear I wasn't going to respond.

I nodded, then managed a, "Thank you."

He walked around to stand in front of me. The concern on his face was clear. It was also the only expression he'd worn since we had driven away from Blaise's house. More than once, I'd wondered if he'd have taken me away if Blaise hadn't told him to.

How deep was Blaise's power? Would he kill Saxon if he didn't obey? Did he kill people with no remorse?

My stomach twisted into a knot, and I swallowed hard. I hated thinking about Blaise that way. The man I had fallen in love with didn't truly exist. If I had known the evil that he was capable of, I'd never have given him my heart.

"Maddy." Saxon's voice was gentle.

He was good, kind, and thoughtful. Why couldn't I have fallen in love with him? It was what Blaise had intended. He'd wanted Saxon for me. He had told me so. How much easier it would have been to love Saxon.

"Please eat and get out of this cabin, walk around in town, do something. Don't just stay inside. Promise me you will. I'll be back to visit when I can. You're safe here."

The idea of eating made my stomach rebel, but I nodded anyway. "Okay," I replied.

"If you need anything, call me. Don't hesitate," he said.

"I will," I told him. "I promise." The smile I managed was weak, but it was all I could do.

Saxon sighed heavily. He was worried about leaving me. He cared about how I was doing. Blaise didn't. Again, if only I could love Saxon. But my heart was destroyed. I'd never love again.

"I've got to meet Dad in Nashville today to look at a horse. I need to go." His tone was apologetic.

"Go, Saxon. It's okay. I'm fine." All lies. I wasn't fine. I would never be fine.

The sad smile that touched his lips made me feel guilty for not trying harder to reassure him. But how did I reassure him of something that wasn't true?

He walked over to me and bent down to place a kiss on my head. "Take care of yourself," he said again before leaving me there.

I didn't say anything or watch as he disappeared. I heard his truck engine and the sound of him pulling out of the drive. The loneliness grew even heavier, and I blinked back the tears that filled my eyes. Setting the coffee, which had gone cold, down on the table beside me, I stood up and walked back inside.

Saxon had said I was safe here, but the fear was something I couldn't seem to overcome. Closing the door, I locked it, then went to check all the other doors. Knowing that the men who had taken me in the movie theater restroom were dead, but that they hadn't acted alone.

Blaise had many enemies. How could Saxon be so sure they wouldn't come looking for me? That they hadn't followed us, waiting until I was alone once again?

There was a dark world out there, full of bad men who did bad things. It was wrapped in wealth and power. My mother had fled from it to save me, and I'd ended up falling in love with the darkest one of all. My heart had seen something in Blaise, and I'd wanted him so much that I'd overlooked who he was. What he did.

When it was your family that he killed, you couldn't overlook it. The fairy tale I'd let myself pretend I was in had gone up in flames.

I was still battling inside over who had left that envelope for me to find. Did I hate them for causing me all this pain? Or had they saved me from getting any deeper into a world I knew nothing about? Who had left it? Maybe if I knew who had left it for me, then I would know how to feel. I'd know why they had done it.

I took time to fold the blanket I'd been covered up with outside, then placed it on the sofa.

Saxon had bought me books last week. They were my only escape—when I could focus on them. Reading would be the only company I had. I knew I couldn't stay here forever, but trying to plan my future was more than I could handle at the moment.

My future was questionable. Saxon had seemed so sure that my life wasn't at risk. Blaise wasn't chasing after me. I was no longer a weakness for him. I understood that, but did his enemies? As lost as I felt, I still didn't wish for death. At least not at the hands of someone who would make that death brutal. If I wanted to end my life, I preferred to handle it. Not that I ever would. I wasn't sure what happened after death, and if this was truly the only life we got before we were dust, I wanted to have a chance to make this one worth it.

Stepping into the kitchen, I looked around at the things Saxon had bought for me. Sitting on the counter, there was a bowl full of fruit, a box of croissants, several different muffins, and the credit card he'd said he left for me.

My name was on the card, and I knew using it only meant I would feel as if I had to pay the Houstons back. They were already letting me stay here for free. Feeding me, getting me a rental car to use. I wasn't theirs to worry about, and I didn't know why they were doing it. If this was because Melanie felt guilty for bringing me into this world and not being there for me when I needed advice, this wasn't going to fix things.

Walking over to the counter to take an apple from the fruit bowl in hopes that I could force it down, I stopped when I saw a white letter-sized envelope tucked under the edge of the bowl. Had Saxon left it behind?

If it had been meant for me, then Saxon would have just given it to me. Wouldn't he?

Confused, I reached for it and noticed my name was written on it in familiar handwriting. My grip tightened as my hand began to tremble. I stood there, holding it, looking down at that script. My chest ached painfully, but that was nothing compared to the inner turmoil going on inside my head.

Saxon must not have wanted to see my face when he gave this to me. I reached out and grabbed the counter for balance and closed my eyes, taking several deep breaths. If just seeing Blaise's handwriting affected me like this, then how could I open it and read it? He could have texted me. Whatever was inside this envelope couldn't just be a letter. It was too thick for that. Was it money? My stomach twisted at the thought. Did he think he could buy me off? From what exactly? Killing my father and brother? Letting me fall in love with him?

Not wanting to look at my name written in his handwriting any longer, I folded it and put it in the pocket of my pajama pants. I wasn't ready for whatever was inside. Would he add a goodbye note to the insult of money? If that was what he had left for me, I was sure whatever was left of the Madeline I had once been would shatter.

"I can't," I whispered to no one.

Unable to move, I stood there, staring at nothing. I didn't know for how long. When the sound of a car door closing caught my attention, I was snapped out of the numbness I'd been allowing to consume me. Moving quickly, I ran to the knife block and pulled out the largest one. Looking at it in my hand, I wondered if I would even know what to do with this. But something was better than nothing.

Glancing around for a place to hide, I went to the pantry and opened it quietly. I stood among the shelves stocked with staples, knowing this wasn't good enough.

Sitting on the floor, I pulled my legs up and curled into a ball until I fit under the lowest shelf in the corner. There was no knock on the door, no doorbell, no sound at all. I listened carefully, but with my heart hammering in my ears, it was difficult to hear anything.

How had this become my life? Hiding in a pantry?

Once, I had been brave. Even when I wasn't sure how we were going to eat, or where we would sleep, or if my dad was going to come home and pay the bills, I was tough. I handled things. But that girl had never known the real monsters that walked among us.

The time ticked by slowly, and my legs began to cramp up. My stomach growled, and my neck hurt from being bent for so long. There was still no sound inside the house.

How long could I stay like this? What if it had simply been someone who had gotten lost or seen a black bear and wanted to go get a picture? The roads in the mountains were narrow, and if someone had taken a wrong turn, they'd need a driveway to turn around in, although they wouldn't have gotten out of their car. Perhaps it had been a package.

My legs were asleep. Staying like this was ridiculous, wasn't it?

Moving as quietly as I could, I stood back up and opened the pantry door a crack to peek out. I listened and scanned the area I could see. It was silent in the house. Completely still with no sign of life other than my heavy breathing and pounding heart.

I stayed still for a few more minutes with the knife still clutched in my hand, waiting before slowly stepping out of the pantry. It was all as I had left it. Nothing was out of place. I started to let out a sigh when a sound startled me. The knife fell from my hand as I screamed. It was while I jumped back away from the point of the knife to protect my feet that I realized it was the sound of the air conditioning unit kicking on.

Closing my eyes for a moment at my own ridiculousness, I cursed. I was losing my mind. I had to get a grip. I could have cut my toes off.

I opened my eyes and bent down to get the knife, then walked back to the block to return it. My attention turned to the front door, and I looked outside the glass window beside it, silently reassuring myself that I was fine. My eyes spotted it then, making me feel even more ridiculous than I'd already felt.

A silver Mercedes SUV was parked outside. Leave it to Melanie to choose a luxury vehicle for my rental car. I had known it was going to be dropped off. Saxon had told me this. Why hadn't I thought of that before acting like I was in a bad horror film?

My phone dinged, alerting me of a text. It was from Saxon.

JUST GOT A CALL FROM THE RENTAL CAR PLACE. THEY SAID THE CAR WAS DELIVERED. SHOULD BE A SILVER SUV. MERCEDES, I THINK.

I texted him back.

IT'S HERE. THANK YOU. I DON'T KNOW WHAT I WOULD DO WITHOUT YOUR PARENTS HELPING LIKE THIS. I SWEAR I WILL REPAY THEM AND YOU ONE DAY.

I saw the dots appear on the screen that he was replying, so I waited. They went away, and nothing came through. He was driving. I needed to leave him alone.

Setting the phone back down, I placed a hand on the pocket where Blaise's letter was tucked.

Eventually, I would be strong enough to open it, but that day was not today.

Chapter TWO

MADELINE

My eyes flew open, and I lay there in the dark, looking around. The moonlight was enough for me to see the bedroom clearly as my eyes focused.

I had been dreaming, but then there was a sound. I heard a door close and footsteps. Even in my dream, I had known something was wrong.

I sat up in bed. I could have simply dreamed the sound, but as my eyes opened, the footsteps were still there. Weren't they? I'd heard something. Was I panicking again for nothing? No. I was sure I'd heard it.

I moved the covers back before grabbing my phone. Then, I heard them again. Footsteps. They were soft, but I was sure I'd heard them. There were a few stairs that creaked, and I knew that sound. Someone was here. This wasn't me overreacting this time.

I pressed Saxon's number, then ended the call. He was hours away from me. Possibly even back in Florida, or … had he come back here? Had he decided after meeting his dad in Nashville that he should come back to me? Surely, he would have texted or called, but then he might have worried about waking me up.

My phone said it was after three.

Tiptoeing to the bedroom door, I stepped out to peek over the balcony overlooking the living room and kitchen. I dialed 911 and held my finger over the Call button, waiting before pressing it in case Saxon had returned. I moved closer to the railing and held my breath, for fear of being heard. There was no one down there, but the light over the stove was off, and I had left it on. My eyes swung to the living room, which I could already tell was dark. I'd left the lamp on in there too.

"Put the phone down," a deep voice said behind me.

A scream tore from my throat, and my phone fell to the ground as I spun around. Huck was standing a few feet away at the top of the stairs. I gasped and covered my mouth to keep from screaming again. My adrenaline was pumping so hard that I felt like I might expire right here.

But it was Huck. I knew him. I had once trusted him. He wasn't here to kill me. I was almost positive he wasn't. Maybe he was. Maybe my knowing about Blaise killing my dad and brother had put me on their kill list. Assuming they had one of those. Why hadn't I thought about that already? Saxon would have warned me, wouldn't he?

"For fuck's sake, Maddy, stop backing up. If you fall over that damn railing, then Blaise will put a bullet in me," he drawled, then held up an unlit cigarette. "Mind if I smoke this?"

I stared at him, but said nothing. Why was he here? If Blaise didn't want me to fall from the balcony, then he didn't want me dead. Yet Huck was here, in this cabin, miles away from Ocala, in the middle of the night. I was confused.

Huck shrugged when I didn't answer and lit the cigarette between his lips and took a long pull from it. "Go back to bed," he said with a grunt.

"What are you doing?" I asked him instead.

He raised his eyebrows, as if that was a dumb question. It wasn't. It was a legitimate question.

"Did you honestly think you were up here in the fucking mountains alone, without protection?"

Yes, I had thought that. Clearly. I had hidden in a pantry with a knife for almost an hour today.

"Fuck," he drawled and took another pull from the cigarette. "You're a naive one. Go back to bed. I'm just headed to my room."

Wait, what? His room?

Frowning, I asked, "Your room?"

He pointed his cigarette toward the room to his left. "Yeah."

I shook my head then. There was no way I was letting him sleep in this house with me. He wasn't Saxon. I trusted the Houstons—well, as much as I could. They were still in the family, but so far, they hadn't done anything but help me. They had gone out of their way to get me somewhere to stay. Huck, however, did what Blaise told him to do. He killed for Blaise. Huck was not a good man.

"No, you can't sleep here."

He chuckled. "Maddy, honey, I've been sleeping here since you arrived. Apparently, you're a light sleeper when you think you're alone."

"You've been here the whole time?" I asked, then added, "Did Saxon know?"

He couldn't have known. Saxon was honest. He wouldn't have kept that from me.

Huck smirked at me. "Yeah, he knew. We take care of our own. You might be pissed about how things were handled, but that doesn't change shit."

My confusion and doubts did an odd thing. They slowly began to churn inside me, and within seconds, they transformed into full-blown anger. Huck was standing there, acting as if my family's deaths weren't a big deal and *I* was overreacting. How dare he?! I had lost people I loved, the only home I had truly ever had.

I took a step toward him as I glared at his nonchalant expression. I pointed my finger at him. "My dad and brother were killed!" I shouted. "I am not pissed! I am … I'm destroyed."

And I was also in this alone. Saxon had lied to me. If he were my friend, he would have told me Huck was here. Saxon was loyal all right, just not to me.

"When you don't know the whole story and you assume shit, then, yeah, that can be painful. Maybe if you'd listened to Blaise, you would understand. But you had to act like a fucking female and run off."

My hands fisted at my sides. I wanted to punch him in the face. I would probably break my hand, or he'd snap my wrist before I could, but the urge was still there.

"NOTHING makes killing my dad and brother okay. NOTHING!"

I spun around to run back into the room I had been using since coming here and locked myself inside. I'd had to get away from him. He was just an extension of Blaise. Every move I made, he would report to Blaise. Just like I now knew Saxon had done.

I was naive. He was right about that. I should have known Saxon and the Houstons wouldn't go against Blaise. They wouldn't hide me from him. Why had I thought they would?

Kenneth was a part of the damn Mafia. They had never confirmed that, but I was sure he was. Saxon would be, too, just like Trev.

All of them—I had let them in. I had cared about them, and they had all been in on this. They'd all known.

Because I had needed someone to trust, I'd believed they were doing it because Melanie had been my mom's friend. I questioned a lot of that story now. If they'd been best friends, then my mom hadn't been real good at choosing friends.

Tomorrow, I would leave. I didn't know where I would go, and I had no money or car to take. The card they'd left me and the rental car weren't safe to use. Their generosity was because they believed I belonged to Blaise. I wasn't a part of *the family.*

My family was gone.

"Blaise would do anything to protect you. Anything. Even before you knew him. He's been doing it for fucking years," Huck called out from the other side of the door.

I paused and glared at the closed door. He was close. Too close. The darkness in his tone wasn't something new, but the words he'd said bothered me. I knew that Blaise had been watching me for six years, but there was something in the way Huck had said it that made me question what he meant. Until I'd been brought into Blaise's world, I hadn't needed to be kept safe.

"Killing my family wasn't protecting me," I shouted, not sure if he was still outside the door.

Luke, the man I had thought was my father until recently and Cole who I had always believed was my brother hadn't been my blood, but they had been my family. Luke had raised me as his daughter, and I was sure Cole had believed, like I had, that he was my biological brother.

Huck said nothing. He had either walked away or he had no response to that. He knew I was right. There was no argument he could have to that simple truth. I started to turn away and walk back to the bed.

"Funny thing about addicts." His voice was directly on the other side of the door now. He was strong enough to open it if that was what he wanted. "They'll do things. Bad things to get that next hit. Terrible things to hang on to what they think they need."

I wasn't going to respond.

My dad and brother hadn't been addicts. They had some problems but drug addiction wasn't one. If that was what Blaise was going to try and get me to believe, he was not going to be successful. My brother might have had a small problem, but it wasn't bad. My dad was an alcoholic. We didn't have enough money for them to be addicted to drugs. Sure, my dad wasted money on his cheap beer that we could have used for essential things, like food. He had raised us alone, without a woman's help. The alcohol was his way of escape from the stresses of being a single parent. I understood it, and I loved him for what he did for us. We were both still living at home and legal adults. Our having jobs and staying there had been to help my dad. At least, it had been for me. They had both needed me just as much as I had needed them.

Sitting on the edge of the bed, I stared at the drawer in the nightstand where I had stuck the letter from Blaise. I wasn't sure I would ever read it. Just seeing his handwriting hurt. I didn't want to miss him. I didn't want to feel anything but hate for him. He had said I was his weakness, but I knew he had been mine. I'd let my guard down and been foolish.

Huck was here. He'd been here all along. Today, when I had hidden in the pantry with a knife, he'd been somewhere. Outside? In his room? Where had he been during the day? He had to have been close if he was here to protect me.

Maybe it was in the envelope. Perhaps Blaise had told me Huck was here and why. It was too thick to just be a letter, and I knew that.

I reached for the drawer, then stopped myself.

No. I couldn't do it. Not yet. I needed more time.

Chapter THREE

MADELINE

The smell of bacon woke me. Not in a pleasant way. My feet hit the floor, and I ran for the toilet. The little that was in my stomach from the day before came up as I gripped the cold porcelain with one hand and held my hair back with the other. When I was finished, I stood up and flushed the toilet, then went to the sink to wipe my face.

The sensitivity in my stomach the past few days had gotten worse. The arrival of Huck had to be why it had reached the vomit stage. Having him here was a reminder of Blaise, which would now be in my face until I could figure out how to leave.

Standing in front of the mirror, I stared at the hollowness of my cheekbones and the dark circles under my eyes. I'd lost weight. I didn't know how much, but my clothes were loose. Saxon had been worried about me not eating, and I had tried to for his sake.

The knowledge that he'd been keeping Huck's presence here a secret hurt.

How many people would I trust and be slapped in the face with it? This would be the end of it. I was going to leave and go far away. Start a life in a place that had no connection to them at all.

Picking up my pink toothbrush that Saxon had bought me only made me think of his betrayal even more. Everything I had at the moment, he'd supplied it for me. I wasn't going to be able to push thoughts of my so-called friend away anytime soon. Brushing my teeth made me gag a little. I needed to eat something. That would help.

I pulled off my shirt before taking the bra I'd left on the back of the bathroom door last night after my shower. No longer being alone in the house meant I wasn't going braless. I slipped it on, then pulled my T-shirt back over my head.

I could still smell the bacon when I walked into my bedroom, and my stomach began to roll again. The trauma of last night had definitely set me off. I fought the nausea as I opened my door and stepped out.

Glancing over the railing, I found Huck standing at the coffeepot. Now that I knew he was here, I was going to have to deal with him. It seemed he wasn't going to do me the favor of hiding.

Getting free of Blaise and his people would be my main focus until I could figure out how to do it. It wasn't like I could walk down the mountain. The rental probably had a tracker on it. Spending the little cash I had that was mine to get an Uber or taxi to get down the mountain would leave me broke.

Swallowing against the bile in my throat, I went down the stairs. Huck looked up at me from his coffee cup as I entered.

He nodded toward the stove. "You need to eat. You look like hell."

I felt like hell. The bacon smell was making the thought of any food sound unappealing. "Why are you in the house? I thought you would go back to being invisible," I snapped.

He grinned. "What, and deprive you of my company?"

I rolled my eyes and headed for the door out to the balcony. It wouldn't smell like food out there. Huck wouldn't be out there either.

"You're gonna eat, Maddy," he said as I reached the door.

I ignored him and grabbed my blanket from the sofa before opening the door and stepping outside to the fresh, cool air. Sighing in relief, I took my spot in the rocking chair and curled up, wrapping the blanket around me. This was better.

The door opening behind me, however, snatched my brief escape right back. Huck walked up to me, holding a plate of food. I shook my head as my stomach turned at the sight of the bacon.

"If you don't fucking eat, I'm gonna force it down your throat," he told me.

I glared up at him. "If you don't get it out of my face, I'm going to throw up, and I will aim it directly at you."

Huck didn't move. He frowned as he stared at me. I turned away from his appraisal to look out over the mountains. Maybe if I pretended he wasn't here, then he'd go away.

"Fuck," he muttered.

Huck then walked away, taking the food with him. When the door closed behind him, I sighed in relief. Thank goodness for small miracles. Laying my head back against the wooden rocker, I pulled the blanket up to my chin and enjoyed my quiet.

After going back to bed last night, it had taken me almost an hour to fall back asleep. My thoughts kept going back to the envelope in my nightstand. I fought off breaking down and looking inside. Eventually, my eyes had closed, and I'd fallen into a deep sleep.

Admitting that Huck being in the house was probably why I'd slept so deeply was annoying. Knowing I was safe from the monsters out there, wanting to hurt me, had made it easier to sleep. I wouldn't tell him that though.

The door behind me opened again, and I rolled my eyes. He was back. Fantastic.

A plate with a croissant was placed in front of me. I looked down at it, and my stomach growled. I was hungry now. Reluctantly, I took the plate from him.

"Thanks," I mumbled.

He set a tall glass of milk on the table beside my chair. I waited, thinking he would leave again, but he walked around and sat down in the rocker beside me. I wasn't going to talk to him if that was what he was after. I tore off a piece of the croissant and put it in my mouth. I'd keep my mouth full.

"When was the last time you had a period?" he asked me.

Frowning, I turned my head to look at him. "Seeing as that is a personal question, I'm going to pretend you didn't ask me that."

Huck rubbed the stubble on his chin while he looked out at the mountains. "Smell of bacon made you sick. You've lost weight. When was the last time you had a period?"

Oh. I shook my head. "I'm not pregnant. I got on the shot. I haven't bled since then," I told him, turning back to the croissant.

"When did you get the shot?" he asked me.

I stopped before putting another bite in my mouth. "Are you serious? I am not discussing this with you," I told him, then shoved the piece I'd torn off into my mouth.

I could feel Huck's gaze on me. Yes, I had lost weight. I didn't want to eat. I had fallen in love with a man who had killed my family. And God knew how many other people. It was kinda hard to eat after finding that out.

"You were fucking Blaise before you got the shot. I'm not asking for details. I'm asking you when you got the damn shot. Did you stop bleeding altogether?"

Sighing, I finished chewing, then met his gaze. "I got the shot about six weeks ago. I was told it could lighten or even stop my period. It stopped it. But before they would give me the shot, I had a period and a pregnancy test. They didn't give me the shot until I had a period first and they were sure I wasn't pregnant."

Huck nodded, then looked pacified with my answer. I went back to my croissant and realized I was hungry. Really hungry. Finishing it off, I took the milk and drank it. I wanted another one, but I wasn't about to go get it. I did not trust my stomach and the smell of bacon inside.

When Huck got up, he took my plate and glass with him before going inside. I stared out over the mountains, wishing he hadn't brought up my period and sex with Blaise. My thoughts were there now, and a lump began to form in my throat. The urge to cry wasn't new. I'd done that several times over the past three weeks. I was torn between hating Blaise for taking my family from me and missing him. I didn't want to miss that man. I wanted to hate him. But my foolish heart wouldn't let me. As much as I wanted to.

The door opened, and Huck appeared again with a plate of two croissants and another glass of milk. I wanted it and wished I didn't.

"You don't have to feed me. I'll get my own food," I said, glaring at the plate of food.

"Eat the fucking food and shut up," he said, putting it beside me and turning to leave me alone again.

I reached for a croissant and realized he'd warmed this one. Taking a bite, I closed my eyes as the soft, buttery taste met my tongue. I should have said *thank you*. No. NO. I should not thank him. For all I knew, he was the one Blaise had sent to shoot my family. My stomach twisted at that thought. I put the rest of the croissant back. The appetite I'd seemed to have immediately vanished.

This was why I was thin and looked sick. How was I expected to look after seeing those pictures of my father and brother with gunshots in their heads?

Chapter FOUR

MADELINE

Thankfully, the book I had chosen was good enough to draw me in and away from the reality I was currently in. I'd spent most of the day reading on the balcony. Alone. Another thing to be thankful for. Huck had only appeared at noon with yet another plate. This one had a turkey sandwich and a banana. He had simply ordered me to eat after placing it and a glass of ice water beside me.

I had eaten after he went inside, of course. My stomach had felt better, and I was giving all the credit to the story I had escaped into. I hadn't been able to read the romance novels Saxon had brought me, but this was a thriller and had me completely enthralled.

When the door on the balcony opened again, I looked up, thinking it was too early for dinner and I didn't want Huck's company. It wasn't Huck. My heart felt as if it had jumped into my throat and blocked my airway.

Blaise's gaze was locked on me as he stalked toward me. A frown between his brows and his mouth a tight line. I should get up and run, yell, hit him, something. Maybe scream at him to leave. Not sit here, but I was frozen. Unable to say or do anything. I hadn't expected him. I wasn't prepared to see him. Not yet. My heart wasn't strong enough. It might never be strong enough.

He stopped in front of me and dropped down to his haunches as he studied my face closely. My breathing was erratic, and I suddenly wanted to cry. He was here. Reminding me of all I'd lost. All he had taken. All I couldn't have.

"Madeline." He said my name softly. Too softly.

Tears clogged my throat, and I hated myself for reacting like this. He was a murderer. He was evil. Yet I was fighting the desire to throw myself into his arms like a lunatic. The part of me that ached for him was too strong. Did that make me evil too?

"How long have you been getting sick?" he asked me.

I stiffened. He thought I was pregnant. I could see it in his eyes. It was as if he had taken a bucket of ice water and dumped it over my head. The sanity I had lost for a moment at the sight of him returned. The tears I had been fighting no longer stung my eyes, and I remembered that I hated him. I wanted to say all of that, but instead, I glared at him.

"Answer me," he demanded in a low tone.

I closed my book and put it down beside me. I needed a moment before I spoke. No emotion needed to be evident in my voice. Blaise would not know how he affected me. When I was sure of myself, I met his eyes.

"Today," I said in a clipped tone.

"You've lost too much weight," he said, softer and with concern, as he reached up and rubbed the pad of his thumb over one of the dark circles under my eyes. "I need you to eat more, baby," he said, and then his gaze roamed over me before returning to meet mine.

Hearing him call me baby felt like he'd reached inside me and twisted my heart. Stupid, stupid girl. I was not his baby. Not now. I should never have been. He was right when he had tried to save me from himself. Except he should have tried harder.

I would not be affected by him. I would not.

"Don't call me baby," I snarled.

The corner of his mouth lifted slightly. "You can hate me. You can fucking wish I were dead. But you're always gonna be mine."

I let out a hard laugh, wanting to shove him and beat on his chest with my fists, screaming out all the pain he'd caused me. "No, I am not."

His hand moved to cup my face as he leaned forward. "Yes, the fuck you are. When I told you that I would do anything for you, I meant it. Anything."

Like killing my father and brother because they weren't perfect. They'd had some issues. He would do that for me? I didn't want that kind of help. He didn't get to decide who lived and who died. He wasn't God.

His other hand slid up my leg, and I jerked away from his touch. He wasn't going to do that. Never again. Even if my traitorous body tingled from the contact.

He lifted his gaze from my legs back to my eyes. "Too fucking thin. Huck said he fed you today. Will you come inside and eat for me?"

I was disgusted with myself. Somehow, I had missed how depraved I truly was, but my body was making it clear to me. Because I couldn't deny the urge inside of me that wanted to go curl up in his lap. The draw to him and the feeling that he could make all the bad go away if I went to him—it was insanity, yet it was there in my soul. Surely, I wasn't that dark and twisted. There had to be a better excuse.

Blaise had become my safe place, my home … and then it had been snatched away in a moment. *That was hard to adjust to,* I told myself. I had trusted him, let myself love him.

He shouldn't be here. I had to find a way to get as far away from him and all connections to him as possible.

"Why are you here?" My voice didn't sound detached in the slightest. The emotions he stirred in me were clear. Even I recognized it.

He affected me, and I couldn't hide that.

"Because staying away from you was killing me, and when Huck called to let me know you got sick this morning, there was nothing on this fucking earth that was going to keep me from you." He reached up and tucked my hair behind my ear. "And seeing you so thin is breaking me. I can't deal with this. I've never been able to see you like this."

I frowned. "When have you ever seen me like this?" I asked. I was positive this was the first time in my life I'd ever been so wrecked.

"Hungry? Too thin? Too many times," he replied. "Too many fucking times."

He stood up then and held out his hand to me. "Please come inside and eat," he urged me.

I didn't take his hand, but I did stand up. Having him tower over me made me feel like I was at a disadvantage. He was also too close. I needed space. Hearing the pain in his voice was more than I could handle right now. It wasn't fair. He wasn't fair.

"When did you see me hungry and too thin?" I asked, not sure I wanted that answer.

He looked down at me. "When your father spent his money on his fucking addiction instead of paying the bills. When you were sleeping in a goddamn shelter because you had been evicted from that piece-of-shit travel trailer he moved you into once. When I got pulled away for too long and came back to check on you to find out you had barely eaten in weeks. You had to tie a rope in your jeans to keep them from falling down. When I had groceries anonymously dropped off at your door and you were so damn hungry that you shoved a banana in your mouth before bringing the food inside." He grabbed the back of my head and leaned in so close that the tip of his nose almost touched mine. "That ripped my soul out. You think I don't have one, but I do. It's black, but I was born with it black. You're the one thing in this world that makes me wish it weren't."

I stood there, staring at him. Unable to form words. I'd been told he had watched me from afar for years before I met him, but hearing him recall things I had tried to forget made it feel different. It made it real.

I remembered when I'd thought someone had accidentally dropped groceries off at the wrong door. I was fifteen and hadn't eaten in over a week. I'd grabbed the banana because I was starving and afraid the food would be taken away at any moment when the person the groceries belonged to came to claim them.

"You can come inside with me and eat, or I can take that mouth. Your choice," he whispered as his gaze went to my lips, then back to my eyes.

I had to stay focused. We would not be kissing. He would not be taking my mouth in any way. Even if he had just said things that he could have only known happened if he'd been there and seen it. He was the reason we'd had food at times when I didn't know where it had come from and I was afraid to question it. That didn't make all the other stuff go away. It didn't bring my family back.

"My dad wasn't a drug addict. He was an alcoholic." I defended my dad. That would keep me focused on the truth.

I needed Blaise to be clear on what he had done. The horrible, unforgivable thing he'd allowed to happen at his command. I had seen the pictures of my father shooting up that were in that file, but that wasn't something he could have done regularly. We hadn't had money for that kind of thing. Didn't Blaise understand that? Had he not considered it?

Blaise inhaled sharply, and his jaw clenched. I expected him to remind me of those photos or argue with me. He didn't because he knew he had no argument. Nothing would make what he had done okay.

"What's it going to be? Are we feeding you, or are we feeding me?" he asked as his eyes went back to my mouth.

He was too close again.

I had to keep my distance from him.

I stepped back. "Me," I replied, then walked to the door.

We needed to be around someone else. Even if it was Huck. I didn't trust Blaise, but there was something deep inside me that made me not trust myself.

Opening the door with unnecessary force, I stepped inside and walked toward the kitchen, not looking back to see if he was behind me or not. I could feel him. My entire body knew he was there. I scanned the downstairs, and there was no sign of Huck. When I actually wanted the man here, he disappeared.

Spinning around, I put my hands on my hips and glared at Blaise. This was his doing.

Blaise tilted his head to the side, slightly smiling at me, as if my angry stance was funny.

"Where is Huck?" I spit out angrily.

Blaise didn't stop until he was almost to me. When I had to tilt my head back to look at him, he shrugged. "Don't need Huck when I'm here. You're safe."

"That is the last thing I am," I said, feeling caged.

I hadn't been safe since I had walked into the Hugheses' mansion and seen Blaise the first time.

He thought he could break me down. Get to me. He couldn't. Not anymore. I couldn't trust him. He was evil. He didn't love me. He couldn't love anyone.

Pushing against his chest, I moved away from him. "What happens when I do something to get in your way? Are you going to kill me next? Put a bullet in my head? Have pictures taken of it?" I yelled as my eyes filled with tears. I hated those damn tears. They made me look weak, and I wasn't weak, but I was hurting. I was hurting because of him.

Blaise moved too quickly. My brain didn't have time to process it to react. He had me backed up against the counter with his arms on both sides of me so I couldn't move. He looked furious. A snarl came from his chest, and in that moment, I could see the killer. He was in there. The cold, brutal monster lurking … but that wasn't all I could see. If it were, then it might be easier to only feel hate toward him. If the pain and regret weren't so clear in his green depths too, then I could hate him completely.

"Kill you?" he bit out through clenched teeth. "I would take the motherfucking bullet for you. Why can't you get that through your head, Madeline? I can't even stand the idea of causing you pain unless it's with my dick stretching your pussy until you can't walk." He ran the back of his finger across my cheek. "I'd like to spank your sweet ass until it's red and tender. I admit that. But kill you? Fuck, baby. I can't live without you. The day you die, they might as well take me, too, because you can bet your ass that I'll be right behind you."

That was not sweet. That was wrong. Telling myself that was one thing. Accepting it was another.

How did he manage to get to me like this? What was it about him that messed me up and confused me? I knew who he was and what he had done, yet part of me had just melted at his words.

My eyes flew open, and I gasped when his hand slid inside the leg of my shorts. This was when I should scream and push him away. Call him horrible names. Remind him of all the horror he had caused. Yet I didn't move.

I stared into his eyes, looking for something dark and twisted to snap me out of it. Maybe I was just as evil. My breath was coming in fast and hard. I was messed up. Maybe my childhood had ruined me. All the chaos I'd lived through had warped me. Made me too weak to stop this.

His finger brushed the crotch of my panties, and I bit my bottom lip to keep from making a noise. At least I could be silent. Not let him know that I was reacting to his touch.

"You're wet, Madeline." Blaise's voice was a low, deep growl.

My legs began to tremble. No! I should not be doing this. It was beyond wrong. This was a line I didn't want to cross. One where I had to question what kind of person I had become.

Blaise picked me up and sat me on the counter. I could use my legs to kick him and get free, but I didn't. When he began pushing my legs open and then stepped between them, I watched him, but said nothing. Did nothing.

Closing my eyes, I swallowed hard and fought the desire pooling in my stomach. I would stop him. Just one more second, and then I'd push him back. End this thing. Run down the damn mountain if I had to.

His fingers slid inside the leg of my shorts again, and I was thankful they were soft knit shorts. Easily accessible and pushed aside. That thought alone made it clear Blaise wasn't the only monster in this room. A finger slipped under my panties, then ran along the slickness. I cried out, then jerked as the spark of pleasure from his touch shot from between my legs throughout my body.

"My pussy." Blaise's deep, commanding voice made me tremble.

He began to rub my clit slowly. Circling it and then putting slight pressure on it. There was no control left in my body. Tears burned the back of my throat at my complete betrayal, and yet I couldn't stop this. I would die if he stopped now.

"You're so wet that I can smell you through the shorts," he whispered near my ear, then bit my lobe before sinking two fingers inside of my needy entrance.

"Blaise," I whimpered, grabbing his upper arms, feeling the muscles flex under my touch.

His mouth pressed a kiss to the edge of mine. It was soft. Too gentle. A tear slipped out of the corner of my eye. I lifted my hips and began riding his hand like it was the actual act of sex. He brushed a kiss on the opposite side of my mouth.

"Mine," he said against my lips just before his mouth covered mine, and being the dark, twisted person I had become, I opened for him willingly.

The pleasure built stronger as the moment of my release drew closer. The taste of mint and cigarettes filled me, and nothing had ever tasted as sexy. Blaise wasn't just corrupt; he was sinful. Yet, wrapped in his package, he made you crave it.

His finger slid out of me, and instead of being relieved and snapping out of this sordid euphoria, I tightened my hold on him, desperation clawing at me.

"Please," I begged him, and I knew in that moment that I was willing to do whatever he asked if he wouldn't stop.

Blaise grabbed the waist of my shorts. "Off," he ordered.

I lifted my hips, and he tugged the shorts and panties down, letting them fall to the floor. Blaise shoved his jeans and briefs down in one swift move, then grabbed my hips and slammed inside of me in one hard thrust.

The scream that tore from me wasn't one of pain. It was complete rapture. I was lost in it. Needing him like an addict needed their next fix.

His gaze was locked on me. "Tell me what you want, Madeline."

"This," I replied, wanting him to move inside me.

He shook his head once. "Tell me exactly what you want, baby."

I kept my eyes locked with his. He was demanding that I admit it. It wasn't enough that he had me spread open for him in less than an hour after his arrival.

He wanted to hear me say that I was as depraved as he was. That I needed to be filled by him like I needed to breathe.

He moved in and out slowly.

"I want you to fuck me," I said, my voice breaking.

His pupils dilated as his nostrils flared. "You want it hard?"

I nodded. God, yes, hard. I wanted it to hurt.

"Say it," he ordered.

Desperate for him to stop the teasing with his small strokes, I let go of his arms and leaned back on the counter, bracing myself with my hands, then opened my legs wider, placing the heels of my feet on the edge so that he sank in deeper.

"Fuck me—hard!" I demanded.

A growl came from his chest as he grabbed my open thighs and slammed into me hard. My head fell back as he used my body roughly. His fingers bit into the soft flesh of my thighs. I was stretched until it burned from the abusive way he was taking my body. Yet I lifted my hips to meet each thrust.

"Missed this," he said with a groan. "Needed to be buried inside this tight pussy so fucking bad."

His words made the frenzy inside me worse.

His hands slipped under my legs, and he pulled them up higher on his waist. "Mine. This is mine."

I was willing to agree to anything if he gave me what I knew was coming. He bent his head, and his tongue thrust inside of my mouth in the same commanding way he was taking my body. I sucked his tongue hard, needing more of his taste. The sound that came from his chest was more animal than human.

The quickening inside me broke free with a rush of pure nirvana as a scream erupted from my chest. "OH GOD!"

"That's it, baby. My fucking pussy." The possessive growl in his voice only made me spasm with another wave of bliss.

"FUUUCK!" Blaise roared as he shot his release into me. His body pumped liquid heat inside me as he jerked and cried out my name.

I opened my eyes to look at him, and his beautiful face looked even more breathtaking as he found his own pleasure. I had done that. I'd made him feel like that. It was as heartbreaking as it was powerful.

When his eyes opened, they were locked on me. He didn't pull out of me, and I was wanton enough that I held on to him. Needing to feel this connection.

"Being inside you is fucking incredible. You make me want to keep you locked up and filled with my cum. I have no control when I'm buried inside you."

I felt my face warm, and I dropped my gaze. The guilt was sinking in. I'd known it would, but I had been willing to face the aftermath for the moment. I couldn't just point my finger at Blaise now. Not when I'd given myself to him, demanding that he give me pleasure. There were no lies between us.

I pulled back, needing to get away now. To face what I'd done. Accept it and find a way to live with myself.

He tightened his hold on me. "Oh, hell no," he said. "You aren't doing this."

I closed my eyes to keep from looking at him. "I shouldn't have done that. I lost control."

"Fuck that, Madeline. Look at me," he ordered.

I shook my head.

"Madeline, please look at me," he pleaded.

"I can't," I replied honestly.

"Why not?"

"Because you make me forget. I'm a bad person. I … I did this with you and …" I stopped trying to explain.

He wouldn't understand. My father and brother had deserved more from me.

Blaise pulled from me then and backed away. The coldness spread through my body immediately. I fought the need to shiver. This was what I had asked for.

When I felt him touch my foot, my eyes opened, and I watched silently as Blaise slid my panties back up my legs. When he reached my thighs, he picked me up and stood me on the ground.

"I can do it," I told him, fighting the desire to have him touch me.

"I know you can. But I don't care," he replied as he ignored my hands and pulled the satin material up and over my bottom.

When he turned and picked up my shorts, my throat tightened with emotion. Too many things were wrestling inside me, and I didn't know how to compartmentalize them all.

Unable to make a decision on what I should be doing instead of what I was doing, I let him put my shorts on me too. When he was done, I stepped away from him.

"I need to feed you. You're too thin," he said as he walked around me and toward the fridge.

"I think it's best if you leave," I told him. Although that was a little too late.

"No," he replied.

"What we did … we shouldn't have. It doesn't change anything. I can't do this with you. My dad—"

Blaise turned, and the desperation in his eyes stopped me from saying more. "Don't. I know what you saw. I know what you think of me, and I understand that. But I can't just fucking walk away from you." He stopped and sighed heavily, running a hand through his hair. His eyes looked at me with so much sorrow that everything inside of me ached. "Let me feed you. Please."

I said nothing as I stared at him. How had this man—the one determined to take care of me with such pain in his eyes that it tore at my soul—killed my family?

"What sounds good to you?" he asked me.

Something he couldn't give me—waking up and realizing this had all been a nightmare. Finding out that the man I loved hadn't killed my family. That I wasn't a dark and twisted person because I had just fucked him on the counter.

"I don't know," I whispered.

He turned back to the fridge. He didn't reach for anything as he looked inside at the contents. We didn't speak. The silence continued, and neither of us moved.

Why did he look so defeated? Even his posture wasn't the same commanding presence that was part of who he was.

"Blaise?" I asked.

"Hmm?"

"Do you know how to cook?" I asked him instead of asking the important things. The things that I knew I didn't want answers to.

He glanced back over his shoulder at me. "Nope."

The corner of his mouth lifted slightly, and I felt mine do the same. I had no right to smile. Especially at him.

"I'll find myself something to eat," I told him.

The almost smile on his lips became a scowl. "No," he replied. "I need to do it."

"I am perfectly capable of making myself a meal," I said.

He swung his eyes over my shoulder toward the door. "Huck fed you. You needed to eat, and he was the one to make sure you did. I fucking hate that. I am the one who makes sure you eat."

No, no, no. Stop saying those things.

I couldn't handle it. He was the monster. He was the thing I should fear most. When he said things like that, things no one had ever said to me, it confused me.

I walked out of the kitchen, needing to get some distance. He would talk some more, and I didn't trust the things he would say. I went to the door that led outside and stared out at the rental car that I hadn't used. There was no other vehicle here.

How had Blaise gotten here? Had Huck left in Blaise's vehicle?

"How do you feel about pizza?" Blaise asked me.

I turned to look at him. "You found pizza?" I asked him.

"No. I ordered it," he replied.

I stood there, looking at him, suddenly wanting to laugh and feeling wrong for feeling that way.

"Why did you do it?" I blurted out.

Even if nothing he said would make it okay, I needed to know. Because this emotional turmoil inside of me was going to make me go insane.

"Order pizza? Because you need to eat," he replied, his expression dark. He knew that was not what I had been asking him.

I shook my head. "That's not what I meant," I replied.

"It's not time to talk about that," was his only response, and then he walked past me.

That wasn't the answer I wanted. "Then, you need to leave. Emotionally, I can't handle this. Please, leave."

He stopped walking, but he didn't turn around and look at me. His hands fisted at his sides. If he didn't want to leave, I wasn't going to be able to make him. All I had was the rental car outside, but if he pushed me, I would leave in it and use the card Saxon had left for me to find a hotel room. I could hope there wasn't some tracking device on the car, but I could ditch it before I got a room. The rest I didn't have an answer for. I just couldn't stay here with him.

"Can't you just understand that I am protecting you?" he asked, finally turning back to look at me.

I shook my head. "No, I can't. Killing my family isn't protecting me. We didn't have much, but they didn't do anything to hurt me."

Blaise looked as if he wanted to say more, but he didn't. Instead, he turned and walked to the door that led out onto the balcony. I wasn't going to follow him. I wouldn't beg him for anything else. If this was the way he was going to be, then I was leaving.

I went back upstairs and grabbed my duffel bag, then filled it with the few items of clothing that Saxon had taken me to buy when we left town. Opening the drawer, I took out the envelope that Blaise had left for me and slipped it into the bag too. One day, I would read it.

When I got back downstairs, I walked over to take the keys to the Mercedes and the credit card that Saxon had left me and slipped them into my pocket. Glancing back one more time, I saw Blaise's back through the windows that overlooked the mountains. He would hear the SUV leave, but he had no way of following me.

I opened and closed the door quietly, then turned to walk down the steps toward the driveway. When I drove away, I would be alone. Fear began to blossom in my chest, and I tried to ignore it. I had thought I was alone once already, and I hadn't handled it that great. This time, I would truly be alone. There would be no Huck secretly watching over me.

Taking a deep breath, I unlocked the car door with the key fob. I would be okay. I'd be careful. Staying here wasn't an option. Blaise wouldn't leave, and if I didn't get distance from him, I would find myself once again back in his world. He'd gotten my pants off in less than thirty minutes. It was clear that I wasn't ready to be near him.

"Probably not your best idea," Huck drawled from behind me.

Closing my eyes and letting out a sigh, I turned around to look at him. I'd thought he had left, but there he was, leaning against a tree with his arms crossed over his chest, watching me.

Damn him. Did he have to be everywhere?

"I have no other choice. Y'all won't leave, so I will," I told him.

He scowled at me, as if I was the one who had done something wrong. "Do you love him?" he asked me.

What kind of question was that? It was pointless. He'd done the unforgivable.

"I did," I replied. I still did, but admitting that made me feel dirty.

"Did?" he asked me, then pulled out a cigarette from his pocket.

"He killed my family!" I shouted.

Was killing so common to them that they truly didn't see how this was wrong? Did they think I should accept it and move on like it was nothing?

"Not technically. He didn't pull the trigger," Huck replied.

"You, Gage, or Levi did it because he had ordered it!" I spit out, feeling sick.

"Yes, it was on his orders, but your life was in danger."

I shook my head. "My life was not in danger. An alcoholic father who wasn't abusive but needed my help wasn't danger. It was fucking life."

"A life you were about to lose. If it wasn't for Blaise, you'd be somewhere in fucking Central America right now. Or dead," he told me, then lit the cigarette between his lips.

"What do you mean?" I asked him.

"Enough," Blaise's voice called from the front steps. "That's enough, Huck." There was a warning in his tone that I already knew Huck would obey. It was what they all did.

"What did he mean by that?" I asked Blaise.

I watched as his jaw worked, and he gritted his teeth. He wasn't happy that Huck had said what he did. It was more than anyone else had said to me. I'd give him that.

"Fuck," he growled and ran a hand through his hair.

"She was leaving," Huck said, defending himself, but not looking real concerned.

"I can fucking see that," Blaise shot back at him. Then, his gaze swung back to me. "Come back inside. We'll talk."

I didn't move from my spot. Not until I knew our talk was going to answer some questions. There was nothing he could say to right the wrong he'd done. I'd never be able to forgive him, but I wanted to be able to move on from this. Even if it was without him. I needed closure.

"Will you tell me why you killed my family?" I asked him.

"Yes, Madeline, I will," he replied.

Chapter FIVE

MADELINE

I sat down on the sofa and waited for Blaise to speak. He hadn't said anything when I came back inside. He'd simply taken my bag from me and walked into the living room, then dropped it on an empty chair.

"Talk," I demanded.

He shot me a frustrated look.

"Why is it so hard to just tell me? I know you did it. I just need to know why," I told him. I didn't say this was for me to get closure. I wasn't sure he'd talk if he knew I planned on leaving anyway, but how could I stay?

"Because my need to keep you safe isn't just physically. It's emotionally too."

Did he not realize killing my family wasn't protecting my emotions? I almost pointed it out, but I could see he was going to say more. I remained silent.

"Well, that ship has sailed," I said bitterly.

Blaise flinched and nodded, dropping his gaze to his hands. "I know."

He was silent a moment, and I thought he'd changed his mind. But finally, he lifted his eyes and looked directly at me. His jaw worked, as if what he was going to tell me would hurt him, which made no sense to me at all. There could be no pain greater than the photo of my family dead with gunshots to their heads.

"Two years ago, Luke's alcoholism became something more. I know because, to keep you safe, I had to watch everything he did, and as Cole got older, I began to watch his moves too. I kept tabs on him and Cole. It was easy enough to stop the street dealers from selling to Luke. One word from me, and it ended." Blaise paused, and the muscles in his neck flexed.

"Luke went to some other places, looking for a hit, but my control went pretty far, and he was shut down. So, he went darker and into some shitty places to find some lowlife dealers that would sell to anyone. I wasn't alerted that he'd made this connection because my feelers don't go into that part of the underworld. I should have watched him closer, but for a moment, it seemed he'd cleaned up. It wasn't until Cole got involved and started selling that I realized what had happened. I'd failed you. I'd not looked deeper and caught it sooner. Luke had encouraged Cole to sell because he needed the money for his own addiction." Blaise paused and ran a hand over the stubble on his jaw as he seemed to struggle to control his anger.

"Luke started using more than Cole sold, but to make it worse, Cole had also started using. They owed a lot of money … to several different dealers."

The darkness in Blaise's eyes was a mixture of fury and regret. He didn't want to tell me the rest. I could see that without him saying it. If he'd killed my family because they had an addiction, then I could understand why he didn't want to finish. That wasn't a reason to kill anyone. I could have gotten them help. If I'd just known.

"Heroine is powerful, Madeline. When people get addicted, nothing else matters. They lose sight of things. They aren't themselves." He sighed, sat down then leaned forward, resting his elbows on his knees. "That's where Luke was. He was gone. The man needed his next fix, and no one would give it to him. He owed money, and his life was being threatened. It was a fucking miracle he hadn't been killed yet. I was afraid that you'd get hurt or killed. I stepped in to see if I could clean his debts up. But he'd already made his own move." Blaise stopped, and his jaw worked as he clenched his teeth.

I was afraid to speak. Whatever was coming next, he was struggling with it.

"The man who raised you, Luke, wasn't your father. You know that. Please, baby, remember that. I need you to keep that in your head while I finish this."

His eyes were pleading with me, but I said nothing. It didn't matter to me that Luke hadn't been my biological father. He was the man who had raised me after my mother died. He could have given me away, put me into foster care. Forgotten about me. Having only one kid to raise would have made his and Cole's lives easier. But he'd kept me. He had struggled to keep us both.

"Luke made a deal. With the biggest sex trafficker in the States. He goes by Uncle. The bastard is a sick man. Luke had agreed to hand *you* over for half a million dollars." Blaise swallowed hard and took a deep breath. "No motherfucker was going to have you, abuse you, touch you."

He shook his head, looking furious. The room, however, had started to spin for me.

"I took Gage and Huck with me. We found Luke and followed him into a warehouse two miles from your apartment.

I wanted to talk to him. Offer to get him out of his situation and get him and Cole some help. I was going to take you after getting them help. Get you moved in with the Houstons and away from that shit life you were in. But Luke refused and pulled a gun on me. Told me I had messed with the wrong people and took the shot. He missed, and it took every fucking ounce of control in me not to put a bullet in him right then. But you loved him, and I couldn't do it. I used the butt of my gun to knock him out instead. Huck and Gage knew about you, but they'd never been sent to watch you. I did that. I was the one who watched you. They were outside, listening, and came running in as Luke hit the floor. I sent them to find Cole, and I was going to make sure you were safe. You were babysitting that day, and I didn't want you walking back to that apartment.

"They found Cole leaving your apartment with two other men. I had instructed my guys to talk to Cole. To only kill him if it was the only way to save you. I was outside the apartment where you were babysitting, watching for any sign that you were in danger. Gage knew my location, and when they started in your direction, they intercepted them, then convinced them to go into my empty apartment, which I kept available so I could watch you closely and in the event you ever needed me.

"Cole was angry and hotheaded. He didn't like that Huck and Gage had messed with their plans. When Gage explained to him that he didn't have to do this, that there was someone more powerful than the people he was dealing with, willing to give him another option, he laughed and said that he didn't want another option and that we had stopped the wrong people. That you'd be untraceable within the hour."

I felt dizzy and reached to grip the armrest on the chair.

"Fuck," Blaise whispered, but I couldn't focus.

I felt him in front of me. I tried to breathe as I stared at him. He looked as if he felt this as deeply as I did.

He took my hands in his and held them tightly. "Look at me, baby."

I did. I kept my eyes on him and finally inhaled air.

"Finish," I told him. I needed to know. As horrible as this was, I needed to know.

He didn't say anything at first.

"Tell her." Huck's voice broke the silence.

I hadn't realized he had followed us inside.

Blaise didn't look away from me. "What they didn't know was that I was shadowing you. No one would get close to you. Huck called me to tell me they were coming. One of the other men pulled a gun on Gage, but not many people are as fast with a trigger as Gage. He took out both men and had it trained on Cole. The door to the apartment opened, and Huck fired at the first man who walked inside. Luke was behind him. Because of the distraction, Cole underestimated Gage. He went for his gun, but Gage was faster. When Cole was taken out, Luke yelled things that you do not want to hear—and even if you fucking hate me till the day I die, I will not repeat them. I won't do that to you. But he pulled out a gun, and after hearing the vile things that Luke had said, Gage knew there was no other option. He took the shot. What Gage did wasn't just on my command. He wanted them dead because it was the only way you would be safe."

I was dizzy. The room was spinning. I closed my eyes to make it stop, but I still felt off-balance. My breathing had quickened, and it was becoming difficult to take a breath.

Arms wrapped around me, and I didn't fight them. I needed to feel some sort of balance. I was starting to feel frantic. I began to suffocate. I couldn't get oxygen. I started kicking and clawing to pull air into my lungs.

Blaise's voice was close, and I felt his chest against me. His arms tightened around me, and I opened my eyes to see he had placed me in his lap. I focused on his face. He was talking to me. His voice was deep, although I couldn't understand him. The panic inside me was still drawing me under.

He pressed his lips near my ear and began to talk softly. "I'm so sorry."

The pain in his voice was what pulled me back.

I gasped loudly, oxygen filling my lungs, and grabbed his shirt in my fists, holding on for security.

"I'm so fucking sorry. I never wanted you to hear that," he whispered, kissing the side of my head.

I closed my eyes as the frantic feeling began to fade to exhaustion. I dropped my head to his shoulder and held on to him.

"She needed to know," Huck said.

"Get the fuck out of my sight." Blaise's voice was quiet, but the violence in his tone surprised me.

I buried my face in his chest, not wanting to look at him. Not wanting to face anyone.

I had trusted my dad. I had been his Maddy girl. I knew things had changed in him the last couple of years, and he was more distant, but I thought it was the stress of being unable to keep a job. I had feared he was depressed and needed help we couldn't afford. Never would I have guessed this.

The lump in my throat felt as if it was going to gag me.

"I tried so damn hard to stay away from you, but I couldn't. I knew having you meant, one day, I'd have to tell you this, and it was the last fucking thing I ever wanted to do," Blaise said, brushing his lips over my forehead now.

I blinked, and a tear rolled down my face. Squeezing my eyes closed, I felt several tears follow it.

Was there a pain worse than this? If I could have just gone on believing they had died in a car accident, would it have been better, easier?

Blaise hadn't wanted to kill them. That had never been his plan. But my dad … no, he wasn't my dad. I didn't have a dad. He was Luke. He had wanted to sell me. My stomach rolled, and I felt a cold sweat break out on my face.

If Blaise had never found me, if he'd never checked in on me, I'd … I'd be in some foreign country, being used by men for sex. Or maybe dead by now, like Huck had said.

My stomach rolled again at the thought, and I sat up in an attempt to get off Blaise's lap. He held me, and I shook my head. I was going to be sick. I had to move away.

"Easy," Blaise said.

I opened my mouth to tell him to let me go when the first heave hit me, and I tried not to get it on him. He moved me then, but didn't let go of me.

"Go get her a cold towel," he said as another wave hit me, and I threw up again.

He was holding my hair back as another came. My legs were weak, but Blaise was holding me up.

"I'm sorry," I whispered once it stopped.

Huck was there, holding out a cloth to Blaise. He sat me back on his lap, then cleaned my face. I let him do it. I needed him to because never in my life had I needed to know someone loved me more than in this moment. I'd only had one family, and they had betrayed me in a way so horrible that I wasn't sure I'd ever recover from it.

"How could they?" I choked out.

"Heroine. It destroys people," Blaise said. "That wasn't the man who had raised you. Try to think of it that way. The drug took over his brain. Everything that had made Luke the man you called your father was wiped from him. The drug took all that."

Would I ever be able to accept that? Believe that Luke was gone? That the decision to sell me hadn't been him anymore? I didn't think I could. He'd had a choice. I couldn't truly believe that drug addiction could make you that cold toward your child. It didn't seem possible.

I recalled that evening. Replaying every moment in my mind. "I came back to the apartment two hours later than usual. Their mom had been forced to work overtime. It had been so quiet. I went to the fridge to find something to make us for dinner."

"I know. I was in the apartment across from yours," he said softly against my head.

"The empty one." It slowly began to make sense. "The one that was never rented out."

Blaise had been there.

"The cops came. The sheriff came before the chili was ready. He told me about their accident. Said how sorry he was while I broke down and cried. Mrs. Miller heard me and opened her door, then rushed over and wrapped me up in her frail, small arms while she spoke with the sheriff."

"You looked so fucking lost and broken. My chest felt as if it was going to explode," he told me.

He had seen it all.

"The rent was overdue, but I couldn't stay in there alone. Mrs. Miller took me back to her apartment. Then, all that food came from those people who claimed to be from the local Baptist church, and they helped me go through the apartment." I lifted my head and looked at him. "The people from the Baptist church …" I said.

"Were damn good people," he replied, but I could see the truth in his gaze.

I'd never gone to that church—or any church. Mrs. Miller had said that was what local Southern church folk did. Except she'd said they normally brought casseroles and pies, not enough groceries to feed an army for a month. It had been him. He'd paid them or done something. All those things that hadn't made sense back then because I'd been too upset to think about it were clear now.

I laid my head back against his chest. Blaise stood up, still cradling me in his arms, and began walking. I didn't ask where. I didn't need to know. For once, I didn't want any more answers. I might never want answers again. I feared them.

The truth behind the lies wasn't always a relief. It could also be the thing that nightmares were made of. Horrific nightmares that would forever change you.

Blaise opened a door to the downstairs bedroom that Saxon had said was the master bedroom that his parents used. I hadn't gone in there at all, and the door had been closed.

When we entered the room, the smell was distinct. Mint and leather. Blaise. It wasn't because he was in here. The room was his smell. I turned my head to look, and a massive four-poster bed sat in the middle of the room. The bedding was a dark gray, and the sheets were black. This looked nothing like something Melanie would choose. It was masculine. It was simple.

Blaise continued into the master bathroom before sitting me down on the edge of a large tub. I looked up at him, then around the bathroom. When my gaze landed on the open door to the walk-in closet, I saw black boots, faded jeans, and a cowboy hat. Items I recognized. They weren't hanging in an empty, unused closet meant for a rental house. There was a closet full of clothing.

"This isn't a rental cabin, and it isn't the Houstons' cabin," I said, then turned back to Blaise.

Blaise shook his head as he brushed hair out of my face. "No, it's not. I had Saxon pick you up because he was someone I knew you trusted. I couldn't let you walk on the road, unprotected. He was the only one I believed you'd leave with," he said, then cupped the side of my face as his eyes locked on mine. "But if you weren't going to be with me, then you were going to be somewhere that belonged to me," he said, then dropped his hand and reached around me to turn on the water.

This didn't surprise me. Not now. Not after all I had heard.

I wasn't sure if my name was truly Madeline anymore. Was I really nineteen? Had my mother wanted me? Had anyone before Blaise ever wanted me? Everything I had thought I knew about my life had been a lie.

I had wanted to hate Blaise for lying to me, but my entire life had been a lie.

I looked up at Blaise. He was the only one who had ever cared. He'd lied to me, but he had done it to protect me. The pain in his eyes even now was genuine. He didn't want me to hurt.

Had anyone ever truly cared if I hurt?

I thought about Melanie and the Houstons. It had all been orchestrated by Blaise. Melanie wouldn't have known where I was or even looked for me.

Then, something else began to sink in …

"Blaise, whose credit card is it that Saxon left for me? It has my name on it, but Saxon said Melanie ordered me one with my name."

He added bubbles to the water. "It's yours," he replied. "Your name is on it."

"I have no money or bank account," I replied.

"I said it was yours. Not that you would pay for it. Can you stand up so I can take these shorts off?"

I stood and watched him undress me. "Who pays for it?" I asked him, although I already knew.

Only one person on earth had ever cared for me. The others had accepted me and brought me in because Blaise had told them to. Not because they cared for me as a person.

"You're mine. Who do you think pays for it?" he replied, then slipped my shirt off. His gaze went to my chest, then to me. "Get in the water. It'll make you feel better."

I wasn't sure anything could make me feel better, but I did what he had said. He was taking care of me. He wanted to take care of me.

When I sank into the warmth, I looked up at him. "The clothes Melanie bought me," I said.

"Yes, I paid for them, Madeline."

How had I not figured that out by now?

I looked back at the bubbles as they covered me. "What about the rental car?"

"Not a rental. Did Saxon not give you the envelope?"

The one he'd left on the counter for me. It was still in my duffel bag.

"I haven't opened it," I whispered.

I was prepared for him to ask me why, but he looked at me as if he could find the reason in my eyes.

"The SUV is yours. Title is in your name. Insurance and registration papers for the vehicle—it's all in the envelope. Along with a letter from me telling you that I would love you until I took my last breath. Even if I had to live this life watching you from a distance, I would always be waiting for you to come back to me."

I lifted my eyes to meet his. If I had read those words, I'd have been wrecked. He had no idea the power he held over me.

"You bought me a car?" I asked realizing what else he had informed me.

Blaise bent down until his eyes were level with mine. "I would buy you a fucking island if you asked me."

I frowned. "I didn't ask for a car."

"No. But you needed one."

I held his gaze for a few more moments before the reality of everything I had just heard sank in. I dropped my eyes and felt the ache from loss deep inside. Not just the lives of the two men I had thought were my family, but their love too. Something I had never had and perhaps deep down I had known that. I'd wanted to be loved so badly that I had made excuses for them.

"I'm sorry," Blaise said again.

"I understand. You saved me from people I thought loved me."

"I never wanted to tell you that. I swore to myself you'd never know. I hated Luke Reese, but you loved him. He didn't deserve you. Neither did Cole. Without you, they'd never have made it as long as they did. But hurting you like this, knowing that the truth would do this to you, that was what I couldn't face. That was what I fought so hard to keep from you."

As I sat there in my thoughts, which I knew were going to haunt me for a long time, if not forever, I thought about the sheriff who had come to the apartment. He'd told me about my dad and Cole's accident. Looking up from the bubbles, my eyes met Blaise's. He was watching me.

"How did you get the sheriff to come tell me a lie?"

A dark smile that didn't meet his eyes formed on his lips. "We have cops, judges, and politicians at our disposal."

I bit my tongue to keep from saying *dirty* cops, judges, and politicians. His world was one I didn't understand. I hadn't wanted to. Living in the dark and loving him had been the only way I could deal with it. But now, knowing that I'd been living in a darkness before him and not realized it, things would change. I had changed.

My thoughts went to those photos left for me at the top of the stairs. Someone had wanted me to see them. Someone had wanted to hurt me. But who? Did I even want to know? Not now. I wasn't ready for that yet. I knew the answer was going to be yet another betrayal. No one who cared about me would have left them for me—because no one cared about me but Blaise.

Chapter SIX

MADELINE

The flight back to Ocala was on a private plane. Huck was driving my new Mercedes back. I was going to deal with that later. I wasn't keeping it, and that was going to be a fight with Blaise. Mentally, I wasn't ready to discuss it. He wouldn't see the issue. Claiming that I was his when we were having sex was one thing. Paying for everything in my life was another. It wasn't equal, and it felt wrong. The amount of money he had spent on me in my life was more than I'd ever be able to repay him. It was overwhelming to think about it.

I slept during most of the flight, which I was thankful for because my stomach wasn't settled today. I'd eaten some toast for breakfast while Blaise scowled. He'd wanted me to eat something more. He wasn't pushing me though. Not after yesterday. I was still accepting the truth.

My head was resting on his shoulder as we rode in the back of the limo that had picked us up at the airport. He had woken me up before landing so I wouldn't be startled. I needed an anchor to keep from losing myself, and Blaise was that for me. What I felt for him went much deeper than love or lust. It was frightening to accept that I needed him like I did.

"You can go get in bed when we get home," he said, kissing the top of my head. "I'll let you sleep before I fuck you."

The casualness in his tone as he said it made me smile. A real smile, not one I had to force.

I tilted my head back to look up at him. The perfect lines of his face and his firm jawline, set off by the green of his eyes, only highlighted the seductive, wicked appeal of his appearance. There was a reason women loved him, even without the knowledge of his power or wealth. It was an unfair advantage he had in this life.

"What if I want fucked first?" The words spilled from my lips before I could think them through.

Since I'd opened my eyes this morning, I'd craved connection. The reminder that I existed and I meant something to someone. Sex wouldn't heal what was broken inside me, but it would make me forget the betrayal. Blaise made me feel alive, important, wanted. Being with him gave me a reassurance that my brokenness needed so desperately.

His gaze darkened immediately. "Say that again," he said.

"What if I want fucked first?" I repeated.

A devilish smile spread across his face. "I like hearing you say *fucked*."

I snuggled back against him, drawing relief from the pain buried inside of me simply from his touch. His hand slid between my thighs, and I uncrossed my legs, wanting nothing more than contact. He'd been careful not to touch me sexually since yesterday. Having his hand there was an unspoken promise to make me forget it all. If only for a short time. To escape into a place only he could take me. Where nothing mattered but being joined with him.

"You wore a sundress." He sounded pleased.

I nodded, but said nothing.

"Open your legs wider." He demanded.

I obeyed as a thrill ran through my body. It felt naughty to be doing this in the back of a limo. It felt public, although the windows were tinted. With reckless abandon, I would do what he wanted. Give him what he asked for.

My gaze dropped to my lap, and I watched his hand moved up my right thigh until he met the wet fabric of my panties.

"Soaked already?" His tone was amused. "Take them off, Madeline."

I lifted my hips and pushed them down until I could kick them free. His hands went to the zipper on the back of the sundress, and as he slid it down, the straps on my shoulders fell until my bare breasts were exposed. I leaned back, and his eyes dropped to my chest. He began unzipping his jeans. When he had his erection free, he slowly stroked it while he looked at me. I licked my lips in anticipation, loving how his large, tanned hand looked, wrapped around himself as he slid it up and down, finding pleasure as he looked at me.

"Straddle me." His deep voice was husky now.

I was ready to do anything he asked of me. I stood up as much as the limo would allow causing my sundress to fall further down my body, then shook my hips enough to make it slip down to the floor. His eyes followed me, locking in on my breasts as they swayed with my movements. I stepped over my dress before straddling him, wearing only my heels. He held his cock in one hand as his other went to my waist and guided me down onto the engorged head.

"Ride my dick." His voice was thick with the same urgency I felt clawing just under the surface.

I sank all the way down until he was completely inside of me. A cry escaped me when I was fully stretched and full of him. I glanced back over my shoulder toward the front of the limo. The opening between the driver and us was closed.

"Fuck me, baby. Don't worry about him," Blaise said, grabbing my waist.

I started to move my hips up and down his thick shaft. The friction on my clit was different from this angle, and I started to speed up until I was bouncing. Blaise leaned forward and took one of my nipples in his mouth and began to suck. I moaned with pleasure and held on to his shoulders while I rode him. Having the control was powerful. I was using his body to get my pleasure. I could feel my release building and bounced harder, forcing him even deeper.

His hands flexed on my waist, and he laid his head back on the seat to look up at me. "Fuuuck! That's it. Ride it, baby. Take my dick." His mouth was slightly open as he breathed heavily, his eyes hooded.

My orgasm was so close, and I wanted it. I leaned forward so that my clit rubbed against him with each move of my hips, and it only took three more rocks before I cried out his name, shaking as the peak of ecstasy crashed through me.

Blaise let out a shout, and his hips jerked as he pumped his release into me.

I fell forward onto him, pressing my chest against his. He wrapped his arms around me, and we stayed like that until our breathing returned to normal. Blaise caressed my bare back from my neck down to my bottom. I shivered from the touch and cuddled closer to him. If I could stay like this forever, then I could live with all I knew. This was a place where nothing else mattered. Sated in his arms.

"You stay like this with my dick up inside you, I'm gonna get hard again, and we are going to have round two," he said close to my ear.

As if that was a threat. The idea aroused me. I wiggled my hips, wanting more. I knew my emotions were all over the place, but when Blaise was inside of me, I belonged. I knew I was wanted. I was loved. As fucked up as it sounded, it was my raw truth.

"Damn," he groaned, then gripped my butt cheeks with both hands. "I'm not kidding, baby."

I sat back up and began to move my hips back and forth slowly while he watched me with lust flaring in his eyes. He wanted me. Seeing him look at me like that was like a balm to my broken soul. I arched my back, and his thickness began growing inside of me. I moaned as I felt him harden and lengthen.

"So fucking beautiful," he said, reaching up and running his hand over my left breast, then to my stomach. "And full of my cum." The grin that curled on his lips was gorgeously wicked.

I started to bounce on him again, and he grabbed my waist to stop me, then picked me up until he pulled completely out of me. I didn't want that. I shook my head, wanting to go again. Blaise stuck his fingers inside of me then, and I gasped as he pumped them in and out, then ran his slick fingers over my clit and then down the inside of my thighs.

He looked territorial as he rubbed his cum on my skin and around my folds. "I want you full of my cum, leaking it from this pretty cunt all the time," he groaned.

"Yes," I agreed.

"Don't leave me again."

His tone was angry, and then he slapped my pussy hard. I jerked, crying out.

"I'll chase you down next time. Pump you full of my cum until you can't walk, much less escape me."

I shivered as his voice took a low, dark tone. I was reminded of the dangerous man he was known to be, but it excited me.

His hand rose, and he slapped at my wet pussy again. I whimpered as my clit pulsed.

He continued to play with me and pump his fingers into me, coating his fingers with the seed he'd left inside of me.

There was a kink to it that made me feel debased and shameless for being so turned on by it. When he pulled his fingers out, he groaned as he looked at what he'd been playing with, then lifted his eyes to me.

"Get on the floor and stick that ass in the air."

I did as I had been told, opening my legs so that I knew he could see his semen oozing out of me.

"Beautiful, filthy girl," he whispered as he slipped his fingers back into me, then ran his coated fingers back until they probed at the tight, untouched entrance of my butt.

I gasped tensing up. .

Blaise's laugh was low and deep. "Relax," he said as he started running his finger around it.

I squeezed my eyes closed, prepared for pain but shocked when the caress made my pussy clench.

Then, he gently pushed a fingertip in and out. "Easy, baby. I just want to play with it. Little tight pink hole. This ass belongs to me too." His voice was hoarse and aroused.

That was enough to ignite the naughty, wanton side of me that had suddenly come to life. Knowing I was affecting him made me want to press for more. I pushed back as his fingertip went in and gasped when more of his finger sank inside.

"Fuck yeah," he groaned. "Dirty little princess."

I did it again, and he started to fuck my ass with his finger. His breathing getting louder as my moans increased.

"Jesus, baby," he said, and then his hands grabbed my waist as his dick slid into my entrance while he continued to play with my butt.

I had his cock in one hole and his finger in the other. It felt forbidden, and the idea made me cry out and beg for more. I wanted to be bad for him.

"Fuck me harder," I pleaded, rocking back to meet each thrust.

"You keep this up, and I'm gonna pull out of that pussy and fill this ass up with my cum," he warned as he pumped into me harder.

His finger sank deeper and deeper into my tight entrance, and I screamed his name, feeling crazed and out of control. This was what I needed. For him to own me. Take me. Make me forget about everything and everyone else. Just this.

"AH, AH, GOD!" I cried out as he stuck two fingers inside my ass and slammed his cock inside me harder.

"Is that good? You like your ass finger-fucked? My sweet girl likes to be fucked." His voice sounded as out of control as I felt.

"Yes!" I cried, throwing my head back.

"Come on my cock, baby," he panted as he held my hips, pumping into me.

His words sent me over the edge, and I screamed as my body jerked with each wave of pleasure that hit me. Blaise kept up his rhythm until my last spasm ended, and then he let out a shout as he pulled out of me and ejaculated onto my skin. The heat of each shot hit my back, the hole he'd been playing with, and I felt some against the back of my thighs.

I fell forward onto my hands but kept my bottom stuck up in the air while he finished. He used his fingers to rub his semen on my skin. I shivered as his fingers moved the warmth down my thighs, then between them, pushing it into my still-sensitive core.

"Nothing fucking hotter than you covered in my cum. Makes me want to coat you in it over and over again. Mark you. Fucking bite you so people can see you're mine."

I turned my head and looked back at him, then moved my hair from my neck to expose it. "Then, bite me," I challenged, and his eyes went from my face to the sensitive skin I was offering him.

"Come here," he said, wiping one hand on his shirt and holding the other for me to take.

I sat up and let him pull me close to him. He nuzzled my neck and wrapped his arms around me. I held on to him, needing the comfort.

"If you want to be fucked, I'm always willing. Burying my dick in you is all I think about. But holding you is enough too. Whatever it is you need, tell me. But don't do anything just to please me," he said, then leaned back and took my chin in his hand. "Fucking isn't love. There's a difference. Fucking you is the only damn time in my life I'll touch heaven. I'm gonna bust hell wide open, but I can live with that shit because I've had you in my arms. You're the only heaven I'll ever need."

My eyes filled with tears, and a sob came from my chest. Blaise pulled me against him, and I released all my broken pieces while I finally let my pain consume me. He was there to hold me while I mourned the life I'd never been given.

Chapter SEVEN

BLAISE

I stood at the bar and poured another glass of whiskey. If this didn't numb the fucking ache in my chest, I was going to have to break something. Maybe there was a fucker I needed to kill.

"How's our girl?" Gage asked as he walked into the room.

I set my glass down with more force than necessary. "MY fucking girl. Not ours. Never ours." I scowled at him.

I didn't need to break him. He was my friend. He just needed to be careful how he phrased shit.

"Whoa, sorry. I didn't mean to set you off. Just wondering how *your girl* is doing," he replied.

"She's sleeping," I replied.

We'd fucked two more times downstairs. After she'd fallen apart on me and wept, which ripped my damn chest open, she'd come inside and turned back into that insatiable woman she'd been in the limo. I knew it was her emotions making her cling to me and that she was craving connection after what I'd had to tell her. But I was a man, and if Madeline wanted fucked, my dick was going to oblige. The fact that she was covered in my semen inside and out while she was passed out in my bed made me feel like a damn caveman. I wanted to drag her into a hole and keep her there with me.

"She has a lot to work through," Gage said, pouring himself a drink.

So far, she was working through it by keeping me buried inside her pussy. I wasn't complaining, but I was concerned. I didn't know how to help her, and right now, all she seemed to want from me was my dick. That couldn't be a healthy response.

"She'll be okay. She needs time," I told him.

He walked over and sat down on the sofa. "She asked about who left the envelope yet?"

I shook my head, swirling the liquid in my cup around as I looked at it. I had expected her to ask that, but then after all she'd learned, I doubted that ranked very high right now. But it would soon, and I needed to have an answer.

"Levi told you that the security company said the three cameras that should have shown us who took the file from your office and put it at your door were all paused?"

I nodded. "Yeah, he did. Fucking infuriates me."

"Can't just be anyone," he muttered.

He was right. It was very limited on who it could be. Right now, the only video feed we had that morning during the time the other cameras had been paused was one of Angel coming down the stairs, going to the kitchen, getting herself some water, and fixing a bowl of berries, then going back up the stairs. And there was no fucking way Angel had figured out how to pause the damn cameras from the control room. Gina had said she was taking a shower, and Angel had backed that up.

"You haven't put a gun to my or Levi's head, so I am assuming you don't think we did it," Gage said.

I shook my head. "No, I don't."

Although I wasn't positive about Gina. She could have figured out the security system controls. The shower cover-up could easily be set into place. She could have turned the shower on and lied to Angel while she did it. I just hated accusing her of it unless I had fucking proof.

"Weird that no cars were seen arriving that morning. I would swear it was Trev, but he couldn't have snuck in here without the cameras outside seeing him."

I'd thought the same thing. Trev had liked Madeline, but it had been lust. He wasn't in love with her. He'd wanted to fuck her. He hadn't had enough time with her to realize how special she was. He wouldn't have done it.

"They missed something. Made a mistake somewhere, and it'll show up. I'm looking for it," I replied, then took a long drink.

"I fucking hope it's not Gina," he said. His tone made it clear that he didn't see how it could be anyone else.

I hoped it wasn't too, but right now, there didn't seem to be any other answer.

"Speaking of, where is Gina?" he asked.

"Not sure. Probably upstairs with Angel," I replied.

I needed her to keep Angel up there. I wasn't mentally sound enough to deal with her at the moment. I had bigger issues.

"When does Angel go to sleep?" he asked.

"I don't fucking know. Why?"

He shrugged. "I need my dick sucked. Gina is a fucking pro."

I grunted and sat down in the chair beside the fireplace. "I don't want to think about Gina and your cock. She's like my sister." Who might have fucking betrayed me.

"Fair enough," Gage replied. "Mind if I have some folks over?"

I threw back the rest of my drink, then set the glass down on the table beside me. "Not in the mood for one of your public fuckfests," I told him, knowing that was what he was after.

"Not even if I have those two strippers over from Devil's Lair who suck on each other's tits and finger each other?" His tone was hopeful.

"It's time you get your own place," I said, annoyed. "That shit can't happen with Madeline here. I don't want her walking in on that."

"You don't have to join in," he pointed out.

"I don't want her seeing that shit in her own home," I told him, growing pissed by the second.

He sighed. "She's moving in for good. We need a place. Where we can fuck, have orgies, parties, that shit."

I laid my head back on the chair. Gage was a whore. He was also ruthless. He could slice a man open, then turn around and fuck some bitch beside the dead carcass. There was enough twisted shit in his head that it made him invaluable. But right now, I wasn't in the mood to talk about his future fuck locations.

"We're having an orgy? Did someone get those strippers from Devil's who fuck around with each other? I've been missing them. What're their names, Kitty and Starla?" Levi asked as he walked into the living room.

"No fucking here anymore. We need a new place," Gage told him.

I didn't even open my eyes to acknowledge this conversation.

"Oh, hey, Maddy." Gage's words had me snapping my eyes open.

Madeline was standing in the doorway with the black robe I'd bought her wrapped around her and her hair damp from the shower, hanging down around her shoulders. She looked nervous when her eyes met mine. I held out my hand for her to come to me, and she did. I took in the sight of her and wondered if it was me I should be worried about. Just looking at her made my chest ache.

She slipped her hand into mine, and I pulled her onto my lap. She pressed her knees together, then tucked her legs between mine to keep them covered. I liked that she was modest in front of other men. Not something I was used to or that I would have given a shit about before. I'd shared women with the three of them for years. Madeline though wasn't to be shared.

"Want to order out? I'm craving barbecue," Levi said. "Unless we're going to a strip club."

"I need my dick sucked. Let's go get some strippers. We can get barbecue on the way," Gage said as he stood up. He glanced back at me. "We'll keep our phones on us."

I simply nodded. I didn't expect to have anything come up tonight, but I never knew. The guys were clearing out, and I wished like hell Angel and Gina weren't just upstairs. Having Madeline all to myself with no one around would be good for both of us.

"You hungry?" I asked her, wrapping a damp strand of her hair around my finger.

"A little," she admitted, then blushed.

I fucking loved that she blushed like that after she'd let me be depraved with her earlier. Jesus, I'd never wanted to rub my damn cum on a woman in my life, yet seeing it on Madeline and shoving it back up in her had made me crazed.

"What sounds good?" I asked her.

She shrugged. "I can go see what we have that I can cook."

Her eyes looked exhausted. She was lying on me like she had no energy left. I'd thought she'd have slept longer downstairs, but she had only been down there an hour. I wasn't letting her go make us food. I was going to feed her. If she'd let me, I'd literally feed her while she sat here, just like this.

"I'll order out. You just tell me what you want," I told her.

"But I can cook," she argued back.

Pulling her legs closer to me, I kissed her cheek. "But I want to hold you. I don't want to have to let you go. If you cook, I can't hold you. So, please, let me do this."

I felt her sink further into me.

"Okay." There was a soft smile on her lips.

If I didn't get her fed soon, she might possibly fall back asleep like this. The fact that she had lost so much damn weight was the only reason I wasn't taking her back downstairs and letting her sleep in my arms.

"Tell me what sounds good," I repeated.

"Um … cheeseburger and crispy fries. Maybe a cookie or if they have chocolate cake," she said.

I wanted to laugh, but if I did, I was afraid she would change her mind. "That's doable. Even the chocolate cake … only if I get to feed you though."

She turned to look at me and frowned. "Feed me?"

I nodded. "You, in my lap, while I feed you."

She scrunched her nose, then laughed. "That's weird, but okay."

I pulled her to me and inhaled her clean, sweet scent. "Yet me playing with my cum leaking out of your pussy isn't weird?"

She blushed again. Damn, she made me smile.

Chapter EIGHT

BLAISE

The next few days, I stayed home with Madeline. I'd convinced her to get on a swimsuit and go out to the pool with me. The fucking bikinis that Melanie had bought her barely covered her up, and I'd made sure the guys knew that when we were out at the pool, they needed to disappear. They had seen her in one once, and that had been the last time they or any other man would see her in a bikini.

Being alone had given me time to work on Madeline's swimming. She needed something else to focus on. Starting with the swimming, and then we'd go to the ranch and get her back on a horse. I wasn't ready to share her with the world again just yet. The sun had given her a healthy glow, and she was smiling a little more, but not often enough. The insecurity in her eyes was killing me. I wanted to make that shit go away. She was mine.

I had even hired Angel's nurse to work around the clock so that Angel didn't come to the main part of the house. She was taken out to the ranch to see the horses and swim, so she wasn't kept upstairs all the time. I also didn't want her to have a screaming fit in the house. It helped, not having her here so that I could give Madeline my full attention. Once Madeline didn't look at me with those big, haunted eyes and I felt like she could handle Angel's being here and sudden outbursts, I'd let things go back to normal. Although the more time I had with just Madeline here, the more I wasn't sure I wanted Gina and Angel living here to be our normal. It was time for a change. I just didn't have the time to focus on that right now. Or the fucking drama that would come with it.

"Trev's here," Huck announced as he walked into the room. "Just saw him drive through the gate. You give Garrett the new code?"

I nodded. I was sure Garrett had sent him.

My father had called my phone twice today, and I'd ignored it. Getting Madeline back had been my main concern. I knew he just wanted details on her. He'd been fucking furious when he found out she'd left and I'd let her go. I had sent word that she was back three days ago, but apparently, he needed proof. As if the fact that Angel was at the big house during the days wasn't proof enough.

Madeline was in my lap again tonight while we watched some dumbass movie Gage had bought on streaming. She fidgeted with her pajama shorts, as if she was trying to pull them down. I pointed at the blanket on the end of the sofa, and Huck brought it to me without me needing to explain. I used it to cover her, and she smiled at me so damn sweetly that I wanted to take her back downstairs. Sharing her with anyone annoyed me.

"I'll let him in," Huck said before Trev could get to the front door and ring the bell.

The sound always upset Angel, and I didn't know if the nurse had put her to bed yet or not. I didn't need her coming down here right now. Seeing Madeline in my lap like this would send her into one of her fits. I wasn't going to leave Madeline to deal with her if that happened. Things had to change.

"What's he here for? You know?" Gage asked me.

"To make sure I have Madeline. Garrett will want confirmation she's here," I replied.

I saw her eyes turn to look at me, and I met her gaze.

"He will?" she asked me, looking surprised.

I nodded my head once.

"Why?"

"He wants you safe," I told her.

She frowned, causing a small line to appear on her forehead. There was a lot she didn't understand about the workings within the family. Her grandfather had been important to us. That made her important. However, her being Eli's granddaughter wasn't what made her important to me. Not anymore. She was mine. That made her the most important fucking person within the family. Even my father understood that.

"Trev," Gage called out, raising a hand in greeting as my younger brother entered the room, followed by Huck.

"Hey, Gage," he replied, and then his gaze scanned the room until he found Madeline in my lap.

"Hello, Trev," she said sweetly. I didn't like it. I fucking hated it. But that was my screwed up shit.

"Maddy," he replied. "You're back. Good to know. Uh, you ready to leave this asshole and come back with me yet?" he asked her.

I knew he was baiting me, but I still scowled at him. He was my little brother and my only fucking sibling, which gave him a sense of security. With Madeline, he needed to tread lightly.

Madeline laughed and shook her head. "No, I'm good here."

Trev shrugged. "Figured, but thought I'd check. Grand Theft Auto isn't the same without you."

More laughter. I didn't like that he could make her laugh. She'd not laughed for anyone but me since we had returned. But my brother was somehow managing it.

"I was terrible at it, and you know it," she told him.

The fact that she remained curled up against me was the only thing keeping me calm at the moment. She and Trev were friends, and that was my fault. I'd let it happen. I had to deal with that shit now.

"But you're damn good company," he replied.

"Careful," I warned him.

He was getting too cocky. I had my limits.

He rolled his eyes, and my hold on Madeline tightened.

"Trev, long time," Gina said as she walked into the room with a bottle of water in her hand. "How's the big house?" she asked him.

He shrugged. "Oh, you know, topless pool parties, the senator fucking one of his whores in one of our guest suites, the usual."

She laughed and dropped down beside Gage before throwing her legs over his thigh. "Good to know things are normal. I hope Angel hasn't witnessed any of that while she's been there," she replied.

Trev shook his head. "Nope. We save the topless parties for the evenings, and the senator keeps to himself."

Gage even chuckled. I scowled. Trev was not that funny.

Trev looked at Madeline, then back at Gina. "You going to be here with Maddy tomorrow night while Blaise is at the gala?" he asked.

I tensed. That was shit he had no business bringing up, and he damn well knew it.

Gina shrugged, then looked back over her shoulder at me. "I guess. Unless the nurse is staying with Angel."

"You'll be here," I said, making sure the warning in my tone was clear.

Trev grinned. "I'll come hang out, too, after I show face for a few minutes."

The fuck he would.

"Dad said you were taking Helena, so I was cleared from needing to escort one of the Morgan sisters. Thanks." His smile looked genuine, but I saw the gleam in his eyes. He knew exactly what he was fucking doing.

Madeline went completely still in my lap. Her body tensed up. That was not something I had wanted to tell her after just getting her back. She wasn't ready for this bullshit after all that she'd had to hear back at the cabin.

"You can go now," I told him.

He smiled at Madeline. "See you tomorrow night."

Huck came up behind him and slapped the back of his head. "Dumb shit," he grunted, then shoved him toward the door.

"I think I'll go back up," Gina said, standing as she looked at me nervously.

"I'll join you," Gage added and winced when he looked at Madeline.

I took a deep breath, trying to calm my fucking temper. Trev was going to pay for this. That entire thing had been premeditated. Gina had walked right into it blindly.

Levi said nothing as he left through the door heading toward the kitchen. When we were alone, Madeline pulled away from me and sat up straight.

Dammit.

"You're taking another woman to a gala?" she asked quietly, but her eyes were focused straight ahead toward the fireplace. They weren't looking at me.

"It's a fucking fundraiser. Who I take isn't important," I said. She didn't understand the way things were done. She had a lot to learn about my position.

"It is to me," she replied after a moment, then turned her eyes to meet mine.

Fuck, I hated the pain I saw reflected in them. I was going to fucking beat the shit out of Trev for this. He had hurt her to get to me. Damn motherfucker.

I reached up and tucked a strand of her hair behind her ear. "There's a lot you still have to learn about the workings in the family."

She dropped her gaze, then began to push the blanket I'd put on her off. "I'm tired," she replied and started to stand up, but I grabbed her waist and held her in my lap.

"You're mine. This gala doesn't mean shit. Who I take to it doesn't mean shit. It's you who's in my bed."

She lifted her eyes to mine again. "That's all you want me for then. To fuck? Nothing more?"

Fucking Trev! Damn him.

"No! That's not all. You're mine! I've said that so many damn times already. Why can't you see that? Don't make this a big fucking deal."

She nodded her head. "Okay," she whispered. "I understand."

I cupped her face and leaned in to claim her mouth. She didn't fight me and gave me what I wanted. The taste of honey didn't compare to how sweet she was. I savored it and ran my hand up her thigh. She parted her legs for me willingly, and when I reached her pussy to find she wasn't wearing panties under those shorts, I groaned, shoving a finger inside her.

"Ah," she cried against my mouth.

I trailed kisses down her neck as she began rocking on my hand. She was always so damn ready for me.

"Uh, boss." Levi's voice reminded me that we weren't in a private place.

I took my hand out from between her thighs and pulled the blanket back over her, pissed that he had seen her like that. I didn't want anyone to see her being pleasured but me. Ever.

"What?" I clipped out, holding her against my chest as she shivered slightly.

"Sorry to interrupt, but we have a situation. You're needed now."

Huck walked in through the opposite door. "We gotta go," he said, not glancing over at me.

Sighing, I stood Madeline up and pressed one last kiss to her lips. I wished I could stay and go downstairs with her. The need to make sure she knew just how important she was gnawed at me. I wouldn't have that chance tonight.

"Go to bed. I'll be back as soon as I can," I told her.

She nodded and turned to walk away. I watched her go, knowing that things weren't settled. She was fucking hurt.

Once she was gone, I turned to look at Huck.

"Do I get to fucking kill someone?" I asked.

He shrugged. "More than likely."

"Good," I muttered.

The rage inside of me was building, and I needed an outlet.

Chapter NINE

MADELINE

It took me hours to fall asleep. My chest ached so badly that I struggled to breathe.

Actions spoke louder than words. Blaise should know that. Nothing he said could fix the fact that he didn't want to be seen with me in public.

He just wanted to keep me in this house to fuck. What was going to happen when he got bored with me? Where would I go then? In the limo, he'd said things that made me think he loved me. I'd thought he did, and with him, I felt safe and wanted. But that would end eventually. Then, I would be alone.

The family thought I belonged with them because of my grandfather, but the truth was, I only wanted Blaise. If I didn't have him, I would leave and go get a job, a place to live, find a life for myself.

The last thing I thought of before I finally dozed off was that maybe I should find my independence now, and when Blaise did tire of me, I wouldn't be left with nowhere to go.

I wasn't sure how long I'd been asleep when Blaise's arms wrapped around me. I'd been dreaming, and Blaise's body pressed against my back felt as if the dream was still happening. The happiness I'd been experiencing before opening my eyes, however, dwindled as reality slowly crept back in. This was temporary. No matter what he claimed, he would tire of me. He would be the boss. He had to take wealthy aristocrats to galas. Have his pictures taken with women of importance. Not some girl from the wrong side of town.

It stung, and my accepting it was hard. The Maddy I'd been before Blaise wouldn't have accepted it at all. She'd have been furious. She'd have left with nothing but the clothes on her back and said *fuck it*. I didn't feel strong anymore. My edge was gone. I didn't blame Blaise for that. It was unfair to lay that at his door. The truth was knowing that the family I had grown up with hadn't loved me. Their betrayal had wounded not just my heart, but also how I felt about myself. Blaise had blamed it on the drugs, but I couldn't help but think something had to be wrong with me.

Blaise's hand ran underneath the satin pink nightgown I was wearing. It was one of the many he'd bought for me. The stubborn Maddy from before would have put on an old T-shirt before getting in bed tonight. Just to show Blaise I didn't care what he thought of me. I didn't need him. But this Maddy was broken. I was insecure. This Maddy had put on something to please someone else. The thought that I'd become this other person made my eyes sting and a lump form in my throat.

When his hand covered my left breast, I arched into it, stretching my body and pressing my bottom against his erection. Blaise didn't say anything, but his knee opened my legs, and he moved his hand down to slip inside the panties I was wearing. Something else he'd bought for me. Everything I had, Blaise had given it to me.

He wanted me in his bed, he insisted on paying for everything I had, but I wasn't good enough to be seen on his arm. It made me feel cheap and unworthy. I let him do all those things. I had done nothing to stop it. Did this make me a whore? Silent tears slid down my cheeks.

The past few days since my return, he had been attentive and sweet. He said he loved me and needed me. I had let myself believe him, but now, this. It was a blow I hadn't expected. Blaise was going to be the Mafia boss. Perhaps he planned to make me his mistress. Could that be what he wanted from me, although he claimed to love me? Maybe men did love their whores.

He shoved a finger inside of me, and although I hadn't been wet, I knew I would be soon enough. My body didn't care about the gala and Blaise's date. It didn't care that I would never be good enough to have a real relationship with Blaise. It had turned on me from the first moment I had seen Blaise. Even then, my body hadn't listened to my head.

His finger slid in and out easily as my arousal grew. He pressed his erection in the same rhythm against my butt. I began to rock with him as I pushed all other thoughts away. I'd give him what he wanted. He wanted my body, then he could have it. For now. I needed comfort, and being intimate with Blaise gave that to me. I'd take it. But this wouldn't be my forever. I would heal emotionally, and when I did, I was going to take back my life.

Blaise turned me over onto my stomach and pulled my hips up until I was on my knees. I opened, knowing what he wanted, and he groaned as he pushed inside of me. Filling me in one hard thrust.

"Fuck yes," he growled and began to slowly move in and out. His hand slid around me and found my clit, then began to rub it as slowly as he was moving inside of me. "So sweet," he said in a raspy voice as he kissed my bare back.

I soaked in the tenderness, desperate for it. Anything to make me feel like I was more than his source for sexual release. I'd trusted my father blindly. I was naive. I couldn't be that way with Blaise. I had to be aware of where I stood. His words meant little. I had to remember it was his actions that I had to watch.

My climax was getting closer as he circled his finger around my clit and began to fuck me harder and faster. I cried out his name and heard my voice pleading with him.

"My girl wants it hard?" he asked, sounding like he was close to his release too. I could hear the excitement in his voice. "You ready for me to fill this hot pussy with my load?" he asked.

"Yes," I moaned and slammed back onto him as I cried out his name. My orgasm hit me so hard that my body jerked several times.

Blaise grabbed my right butt cheek in his hand and let out a groan. "Fuck yes! Take it," he yelled as he began to shoot inside of me.

He continued to move in and out slowly until I could feel his warmth leaking down the inside of my thighs. When he finally pulled free from me, I fell limp onto the bed.

He moved to lie beside me again, covering up our bodies and pulling me to his chest. Exhausted and sated, I fell back to sleep quickly.

I was alone in bed when I opened my eyes again. Stretching, I felt the stickiness between my legs from last night and decided to go get in the shower before I did anything else. Throwing back the covers, I walked to the bathroom, and the light came on. I glanced at my reflection in the mirror to see my hair a tangled mess, but the dark circles under my eyes were fading.

A wave of nausea settled over me, and I frowned, unsure of why that was happening again. I'd just gotten up, and I hadn't had time to think about my life. No reason to get upset so early. Stepping into the shower, I turned on the warm water and waited until it felt good before I stood under it.

My eyes were closed, and water was running over my face and hair when I heard the shower door open. Snapping my eyes open, I turned to see a naked Blaise joining me. He smirked at me as he wrapped his arm around my waist while he stood behind me. I leaned back onto his chest, needing his warmth.

"Good morning," he said near my ear.

"Good morning," I replied.

"I was disappointed that you were washing my cum off your body until I saw you standing naked under the shower. That view made me see things differently," he said.

"Hmm, I was sticky."

"I'll clean you up," he whispered, then reached for the body wash and poured some into his palm.

I held my breath as he began rubbing it on my stomach and breasts. My nipples hardened under his touch, and he lingered there longer before moving lower until he was washing the insides of my thighs. I trembled slightly as I watched him kneel in front of me and wash my calves and feet before he stood back up and got more body wash in his hand, then moved to do the same to my backside. He enjoyed washing my bottom and spent more time there than necessary, then moved down the backs of my thighs.

When he stood back up, he turned me to face him. I realized his touch had eased my nausea. Maybe it was my insecurities that had been causing it. If that was the case, I needed counseling. This wasn't healthy. Finding my own place and being independent might be all that could help me. Staying here and letting Blaise take care of me was just going to make me feel worse as time went on.

He reached for my right leg and pulled it up to his side, leaving me open. I grabbed his arms for support as he slid inside of me slowly. "I was just going to bathe you, but I can't seem to keep my dick out of you," he growled.

That was his weakness. Wanting to fuck me.

Our wet bodies slapped against each other. Blaise reached for my other leg, and I wrapped my arms around his neck when he picked me up and turned to press my back against the stone wall. He pumped into me harder, then lowered his head until his lips were on the curve where my neck and shoulder met. I gasped at the sharp bite of his teeth, and the pain ignited my orgasm.

"BLAISE!" I screamed out his name and held on to him as the pleasure washed over me.

When he finally stopped biting me, his eyes locked with mine. There was a fierce look on his face as he slammed into me hard before he threw back his head and shouted out my name as he came inside me. I buried my face in his chest and wished this were different. That I could have him in all ways, not just with sex.

He tightened his hold on me and took me with him as he sat down on the stone bench beside us. I stayed in his lap as the water ran over our bodies and his breathing returned to normal.

"I need to feed you. I've got to stop fucking you constantly," he said. "But, damn, it's all I want to do."

I snuggled up tighter to his chest. He wanted me.

Blaise Hughes was a cold, terrifying killer. With me, he was different. I had a part of him no one else got. That should be enough.

But it wasn't.

Chapter TEN

MADELINE

I didn't bother covering up the bite mark Blaise had left on me. Every time he looked at it, his eyes got territorial and possessive. He was downstairs, getting dressed to go to a gala at the club to raise money for a facility that cared for retired racehorses. He hadn't brought up the fact that he was taking another woman with him as his date or tried to explain it to me again, and I hadn't asked.

After I'd managed to eat some toast and berries at breakfast, I'd spent the day reading while he worked. But my mind hadn't been on the book. I'd made a plan. I was going to deal with it tomorrow. I didn't have the energy today. But I was going to get a job, and if that had to be at Hughes Farm again, I was okay with that.

I just needed an income. When I had enough, I was going to rent somewhere to live. I would tell Blaise he could help me choose a place since my safety was an issue. Although I didn't know how his enemies knew about me since we were never seen together. But they did. The kidnapping at the theater had proven that. Regardless, there had to be a place I could live safely.

That was plan A. If he refused that idea, then I'd still get a job. I had to pay for my things. If he was going to just use me to keep him satisfied in his bed, then I couldn't accept things from him. That would make me a whore. I was not a whore. I wasn't going to act like one. I drew the line at that.

"Want a drink?" Gina asked me as she sank down onto the sofa across from the chair I was curled up in, secretly plotting my future while holding a book in my hands.

"I'm good, but thank you," I told her.

She nodded, then raised her eyebrows when she saw my neck. I had put on a pair of black shorts with hot-pink polka dots on them and a hot-pink tank top today.

"Looks like someone got excited," she said, grinning.

I smiled, but said nothing.

She glanced around, then leaned forward. "Seriously though, are you good with this? Tonight?" she whispered.

No, I wasn't good, but that didn't matter.

I shrugged. "I don't think it matters."

She frowned and leaned back with a sigh. "Yeah. Sucks though."

"Yep," I agreed, then dropped my gaze back down to my book.

I heard his footsteps before he appeared, but I didn't look up. I feared how I would feel, seeing him in a tux, looking like every woman's fantasy, knowing he was going to have another woman on his arm. He would touch her back and hold her while they danced. The jealous knot in my stomach was so twisted up that it hurt.

"Guys already left," I heard Gina say. "Huck said he'd see you after."

I still didn't look up. I couldn't bring myself to do it. I knew how devastatingly beautiful he looked in a tuxedo. I didn't want to be reminded. I was sure his date would be stunning, wearing a dress that would turn heads. While I sat here with my hair in a ponytail, dressed like a nineteen-year-old. Even my feet were bare.

"Madeline," Blaise said.

I sighed, knowing he was going to expect me to speak to him. After all, I'd acted fine all day. I'd fucked him in the shower, eaten beside him at the table. I was fine with all of this, like a good little girl, I thought sourly.

Forcing myself to appear pleasant, I lifted my gaze from the book and looked up at him. It was hard to breathe. His blond hair was pulled back in a bun, and the tuxedo made him appear like the Greek god I was sure he'd descended from.

"Yes?" I asked with a smile I hoped looked real.

He stared at me a moment, then walked over to stand in front of me.

"You leaving?" I asked as if I didn't care.

"Yes," he replied with a frown between his eyebrows.

"Have a good time," I replied.

His gaze went to the bite mark he'd left on me. I felt goose bumps cover my arms and wished they hadn't. He'd see them too. Dang it.

"This is just how things need to be," he told me even though I hadn't mentioned it.

I nodded. "Yeah, I got that last night." I finished it with a smile.

He didn't look pleased. I held his gaze until he bent down and put his hands on the armrests, caging me in.

"Then, why aren't you standing up to give me a kiss?"

Because I want to currently jerk that damn bun out of your hair and slap your face. I was so angry. I didn't say that though.

"I didn't know that was expected of me," I replied. "I'm new at this. I've never shared a boyfriend before. I don't know the rules." I couldn't help it. There was only so much I could control. Right now, my mouth was working on its own.

His eyes flared, and I knew what I had said was sarcastic, but I was not dealing well with this, and he needed to get out of here. I wasn't sure how much longer I'd go without cracking and doing exactly what I had imagined doing.

He grabbed my arm and pulled me to stand with more force than necessary. "That's not what you're fucking doing," he growled, as if he had a reason to be angry.

He had me to fuck whenever he wanted and a line of women to date whenever he desired.

"Again, this is new to me," I informed him. "And you're hurting my arm. If you wouldn't mind easing up on it a little."

His jaw clenched, and he let go of my arm. "I've got work to handle. I can't deal with this shit right now."

I shrugged. "Go, work. This shit will stay right here, like a good girl."

"Madeline!" It was a warning. I knew it was.

I blinked, looking as innocent as I could, and stared up at him.

He inhaled sharply. "We will finish this tonight."

"Okay," I replied.

Although if he thought he was going to crawl in bed with me and fuck me after dating another woman, he was mistaken. I did have some limits. Last night, I'd been dealing with the fact that I had lived a lie my entire life and Blaise was all I had in this world. But today, as I had sat here with my book and my thoughts, I'd realized I was stronger than that. I loved him. That was the only reason I was standing here, taking this. But he could push me too far. And I was feeling pushed right now.

He didn't kiss me. Instead, he walked away, leaving me standing there. I waited until he was out of the room before sighing and dropping back into the chair. My heart hurt, I was nauseous again, and I felt like a child he was growing weary of.

"Damn, you're tough," Gina whispered.

She had no idea how wrong she was. I used to be tough. Not so much anymore. I was in a man's house with a book while he was on a date with another woman. This was not tough. This was just pathetic.

We stayed silent until a chime went off, alerting us that the back door leading into the garage had opened. He was gone.

"Want to eat ice cream and watch a movie? Trev said he'd come, but honestly, unless Garrett lets him leave, that's not a sure thing."

I looked toward the door that led to the stairs going to the third floor. "Where is Angel?" I asked.

"She had a bad day. The nurse gave her Valium. She'll be out until the morning."

I had yet to see her since I had come back. I wondered if that was on purpose. Seeing me never made her happy. Another reason I should find a different place to live.

"Since Blaise is openly dating other women and no one ever sees me with him, wouldn't I be safe now? I mean, I could live somewhere else. Get a job and not have to worry about being abducted or killed."

Gina shook her head. "Nope. Just because he takes other women out in public, you're still not safe. You are Eli's granddaughter. You're part of the family. If I didn't live here, I'd have to live at the ranch. I can't live on my own either. The women in the family have to be protected."

That wasn't what I'd wanted to hear. Some hope that I could leave here and get a life without a fight would be nice.

Sighing, I looked back down at the book in my lap. I had no idea what this was about. I hadn't turned the page in over an hour. Gina was sitting on the sofa with the remote, not saying anything more, and I was lost in my planning again.

Another sound went off, and Gina sat up straight with a frown on her face.

"Uh, that's not good," she said, then jumped up. "I'm going to go look at the security cameras."

I followed her into the kitchen and went to get a water while she went to see who had come through the gate.

"Trev is here already," she said, calling out from the area where the security screens were. "What the hell? The gala hasn't even started."

I smiled. Trev was a rebel. He looked for trouble. I took a bottle of water from the fridge and waited for our visitor to make it inside. At least he would entertain me, and maybe I could think about anything other than Blaise and his date. Being with Trev was easy. He was nothing like Blaise. The two Hughes brothers could not be more different if they tried.

The sound of the door opening and closing brought a smile to my face. I hoped he was planning on staying.

"Costume change," Trev said as he walked into the kitchen, dressed in a tuxedo and carrying a long, fancy-looking box.

I frowned at the box, not sure what he meant. "What are you doing here already? Causing trouble?"

He wagged his eyebrows. "Oh, you have no idea. And the best part is, I'm just following my dad's orders."

Confused, I looked at the box he was holding.

He held it out to me. "Go get changed, gorgeous. Garrett Hughes has commanded it. And we here in the family do what the boss says, and Blaise ain't the motherfucking boss yet. Even if he acts like it."

"Oh shit," Gina said, her eyes wide. "Fuck, why can't I go watch this?"

I stared at the box, then Trev. "What is it that he commanded?"

Trev's grin looked almost evil. "Dad wants you at the gala. I believe his exact words were"—Trev cleared his throat and lowered his voice—" 'Trev, take the dress and go get Madeline. She is family and Eli's granddaughter, for fuck's sake. She will mingle within our circle. If your brother refuses to obey me, then you get to do the honors.' " When he finished, he shoved the box at me. "Go get ready. We have a gala to get to."

"Oh damn, oh damn, oh damn, this is gonna be good," Gina said, sounding almost giddy.

I took the box from Trev. "I'm supposed to go to this gala with you … and Blaise doesn't know I'm coming?" I needed clarification.

"Oh, yeah," he replied, looking mischievous.

"Garrett wants me at this gala, and Blaise knew that?"

Trev nodded again.

The fact that my not being there with Blaise was all his doing and not his father's made his taking another woman that much worse. Part of me had held on to the belief that he *had* to take someone else. He'd said as much. But Garrett hadn't ordered that. Blaise did not want me there with him. This wasn't about my safety. Blaise was ashamed to be seen with me.

Well, fuck Blaise Hughes. I was good enough to screw, but not to be seen with in public. I'd show him. I could dress up and look just as fancy as his date or anyone there. Just because I had grown up poor didn't mean I couldn't compete.

"This won't take long," I told Trev as my hurt began to turn into a much more powerful, ugly thing. Revenge.

"Oh, wait," Trev called out as I turned away. I looked back at him, and he held out a bag. "Shoes and jewelry," he said.

I took the bag from him.

"You want me to do your makeup? And cover up that bite mark?" Gina asked hopefully.

I rarely wore makeup. I nodded. "Please."

She clapped her hands together. "This is like Cinderella, except instead of having the handsome prince fall in love with her, she's going to slap the devil in the face."

Trev burst out laughing as I headed to get dressed.

Chapter ELEVEN

MADELINE

"Stop fidgeting. You look fucking incredible. I gotta hand it to Dad. When he wants to make a statement, he fucking makes one," Trev said to me as he took my hand and slipped it through the crook of his arm.

I took a deep breath and prepared myself. This could get ugly, but I doubted it would in public. "He won't kill you, will he? Or me?" I asked Trev, not sure exactly how worried we should be about Blaise's reaction to this.

Trev chuckled. "No. He won't kill us. He'll want to fucking strangle me, but he won't. Dad won't let him."

"But if he kicks me out, can I sleep in the pool house?" I asked.

Trev laughed again. "You'll be fine. Blaise won't kick you out. He should have brought you tonight. This is payback. Enjoy it." He paused and scanned my body. "Because there isn't going to be a woman in there that compares to you."

That was sweet of him, but it didn't help my nerves. I had been set on revenge at the house, but now that I was here, I wasn't so sure. I shouldn't be here. Blaise didn't want me here, and now that I knew he had defied his father by not bringing me, it was an issue. One we had to deal with, just not here. We needed to do that in private.

"Here we go," Trev said as he placed a charming smile on his face and we walked into the large ballroom.

People were dancing while others were in groups, talking. Drinks were in everyone's hands. It was similar to the only other gala I had attended, except the dancing was happening with cocktail time. Perhaps this wasn't a sit-down dinner event. I hoped not. I wasn't sure I could eat.

"There's Dad," Trev said, and I let him lead me over to the group standing with Garrett.

When Garrett's eyes landed on us, he did a quick take of my dress and gave me a pleased smile. At least the boss was happy with me.

"It seems my youngest son has arrived with the belle of the ball," Garrett said a little too loudly.

He held out his arm for me to take, and Trev nudged me. I let go of Trev and walked over to Garrett. He took my hand and tucked it into the crook of his arm.

"This stunning beauty is Madeline Marks, Eli's granddaughter," he announced to those he was standing with.

He'd used my grandfather's last name instead of Reese. It felt odd, but I was grateful. Reese was a name I no longer wanted to carry. I had never known my grandfather, but he had died, wanting me. Luke had not.

I could feel other eyes on me, but I didn't move my attention from the group in front of me. I was not ready to face Blaise. He was here, and he was looking at me. I could feel it.

"Madeline, dear, this is Gunther Ford and his wife, Audrey. They will soon have the largest racing empire in the world at the rate things are going," Garrett said, and everyone chuckled, as if he was telling a joke.

I smiled and returned their greeting.

"Absalon Daniels and his son, Francis. Absalon owns several television networks, and his son is available if mine doesn't snatch you up." Garrett once again got laughter from the others.

Francis was attractive in that *frat boy* kind of way. He gave me a smile that made me slightly uncomfortable. I managed to return it but decided I'd keep my distance from him. He gave me a bad vibe.

"Edger Warren, a banking executive who is currently in between wives. Edger, she's too young for you."

Again, more laughter.

Garrett patted my hand. "I'm pleased you came," he said to me. "Trev, why don't you take our Madeline to get a drink and meet some others here?"

Although he had a pleasant smile, I could almost feel his unspoken words to Trev. It was as if he was encouraging him to defy his brother. That he was in control and this was to be handled his way. Trev placed a hand on my lower back. The back of the dress dipped all the way down to my waist, leaving my back exposed. It felt weird, having someone other than Blaise touch my bare skin.

Trev leaned into me. "Francis is a fucking pussy. Stay away from him."

I nodded. "I already planned on it."

"Dad knows Blaise would kill him. Maybe that's why he did it. Not sure where we stand with the Daniels right now. Perhaps that relationship is about to be terminated. They don't tell me shit."

I hoped *terminated* didn't mean murdered. I didn't know them or particularly like the guy from our brief introduction, but I didn't see a reason to kill them. Perhaps terminated didn't always mean murder in this group.

"Showtime," Trev said under his breath, and I felt him tense up.

My eyes shifted from him to see Blaise standing across the room. His gaze was locked on me, and although there was a room of people between us, I could feel the fury rolling off him in waves. I stopped walking. My heart started to race, and I realized this was a game I didn't want to play. Saxon had said once that he didn't want to get between Garrett and Blaise Hughes. I understood that now. It was a terrifying feeling.

"You're fine. His head might explode at any moment, but he's not going to do anything to you," Trev said. "Now, me? Well, it's possible he's going to try and kill me, but I trust Dad to keep me alive. This was his idea."

My gaze went to the woman beside him. Her hair was black, and her olive complexion with her pale blue eyes was an exotic combination. The dress she was wearing clung to her curves. She was holding on to Blaise's arm as she spoke to the people with them. Jealousy gnawed in my gut. He hadn't wanted me here on his arm, and I could see why when he could have someone who looked like that. She definitely made an impression.

Kudos, Blaise.

I tore my gaze from them and looked back up at Trev. "I need a drink," I told him.

"As you wish," he replied and led me in the opposite direction of Blaise and his date.

When a server came up to us, Trev reached for two glasses of champagne and handed me one. "Let's go find Sax," he told me.

That sounded good. I needed to be surrounded by my friends. I might be upset with Saxon for lying to me and not telling me about the cabin being Blaise's, but at this moment, he was the lesser of the two evils. What he had done did not compare to what Blaise might do.

"He's not going to fuck her," Trev said, leaning down to my ear.

The image those words stirred in me made my stomach rebel. I didn't take a drink of the champagne, for fear it would come back up. I shouldn't have come here. I hadn't needed to see that. I was never going to get over this. How could I? Knowing I wasn't enough. That he needed someone like that to be seen with in public.

Every insecurity I'd ever had was roaring to life, and my head started to pound.

"Madeline, honey, you look breathtaking. Where did you find that dress?" Melanie was suddenly in front of us, beaming at me.

I'd never called her, and when I looked at her now, I felt like she had never truly planned on developing a relationship with me.

"Garrett. He's got good taste," Trev replied for me.

Melanie's eyes widened. "Yes, he does," she agreed, then reached for my empty hand and squeezed it. "When you want to talk, I'm here. Know that."

I didn't know that. She'd barely spoken about my mom to me, no matter how hard I had tried to get her to do it.

But I nodded. "Okay," I replied, knowing I never would.

She glanced at Trev for a moment, then back at me. "You've seen how things are done. It's a well-oiled machine that I know is difficult to embrace if you haven't grown up inside of it. Etta ..." She paused, looking nervous. As if she was going to confide something and changed her mind. "She never really understood it either."

I didn't have a moment to say anything or figure out a way to get her to explain what she meant about that because Trev was ready to end the conversation.

"Sax," Trev called out, and I looked over to see Saxon and Declan standing with some other familiar faces.

Declan smiled, but had a slight frown when she saw me on Trev's arm.

Melanie glanced back and then back at us with a smile. "Go mingle. Have fun. You belong here," she said, then gave me one last smile before walking away.

"You looked like you needed saving," Trev said under his breath, but I wondered if he had thought Melanie was going to say something she shouldn't.

I trusted no one anymore. That part of me was damaged, and every day that passed, it seemed to take even more hits. Reminding me that I could only trust myself.

"How are they part of the family? Or are they?" I asked him bluntly.

"The Houstons?"

I nodded.

"The Houstons have been inside the family and loyal to the Hughes for over eighty years. It goes back to our great-grandfathers. Melanie, however, has too. Her father has been inside of the family since he and my grandfather became friends in high school. Much like Gage and Blaise."

We were almost to Saxon and the group with him when Trev beamed a bright smile at them and stopped talking.

"Wow, you, uh, brought Maddy," Saxon said, his eyes wide as we approached them. He looked from me to Trev, then back toward where I knew Blaise was standing with his exotic beauty.

"Dad loves me the most," he informed Sax and took a long drink.

"I fucking hope so," Sax replied, his eyes going back to where Blaise was. I wished he'd stop doing that. "You're gonna need someone to pay for your funeral."

Trev chuckled. "He'll keep me alive."

Saxon's frown deepened. "You might want to run to him now then. Because death is currently headed this way."

I stiffened, but I didn't turn to look. I glanced at Declan, whose eyes were wide with excitement as she looked behind us.

"Took longer than I thought," Trev said and shrugged. "Heads-up, guys. It's about to get fun. Hughes family drama for your evening entertainment."

Saxon cut his eyes at Trev. "You're crazy."

Trev placed his hand on my lower back, and I closed my eyes tightly. This would be okay. I needed to calm down. Blaise was territorial, but I was not his date. His dad had bought the dress, shoes, and diamonds I was wearing. Not Trev. Technically, Trev and I were doing a job for the family.

"Shiiit," one of the guys I remembered from the pool party said in a low voice. "You've got the biggest balls I've ever fucking seen."

Trev held up his glass. "Sure do."

"Remove your hand." Blaise's voice was low and hard.

I took a deep breath and bit my bottom lip. Saxon looked at me with fear in his gaze, which did not help. Trev, however, left his hand on my back. It suddenly felt like hot coals. I was tempted to take it off myself. For Trev's safety and mine.

"Hey, brother. I'm sure you'll understand that I am doing what our father ordered me to do. Maybe you should take that temper of yours and go talk to dear ol' Dad," Trev said, then took a sip of his drink.

"You stepped into a ring you shouldn't have." Blaise's threat was clear.

Saxon tensed, and I felt like I might be sick.

Trev needed to just drop his hand. That was all. Nothing was said, and I didn't look at them to see what silent communication was happening, but Trev's hand finally moved away from me, and I let out the breath I'd been holding.

"Madeline, come," Blaise ordered me.

Every eye was on me. What was I to do? Go with Blaise? What, and let him walk me outside and put me in a car to send me home? That was humiliating, and he would do it. I knew he would. I'd defied him, and he didn't like being defied. I wasn't sure I would be going back to his house after this. The Houstons weren't going to let me come back. They'd be too scared. They clearly did what Blaise told them to do. But Garrett had put me in this position, so maybe he'd let me go to the big house or the pool house, like I'd mentioned to Trev.

I finally turned to look at Blaise. He wasn't going to hurt me. At least, I didn't think so. He was just possessive, and although he had a gorgeous date, he didn't like me being here with Trev. It wasn't fair, but I was beginning to think Blaise didn't care about fair.

"Hello, Blaise," I said, forcing a smile. "It seems your father wanted me here, and since his oldest son had a date, he asked his younger son to bring me. He even bought the dress." I tried to keep my voice light, as if this were funny and he should laugh.

Blaise's jaw worked as he clenched his teeth. He didn't think it was funny.

"She's not lying. Even the diamonds came from the safe. Dad picked them out," Trev said beside me.

"Come. Now," he said through clenched teeth.

I glanced over to where I'd seen Garrett last, and he was watching us closely. When my eyes met his, he excused himself from those he was with and started walking in our direction.

"And here comes Dad," Trev said beside me.

The expression on Blaise's face would terrify most people. However, his brother seemed not at all concerned. I was still trying to decide if I should be worried.

"Your dad is coming," I told Blaise. "You have a stunning date." Saying those words was painful, and I had to swallow the lump in my throat. "I did what I was told. Trev did what he was told. It's family business, right?" I said with a lift of my shoulders, trying to calm him down.

"Blaise." Garrett's tone, although calm, made it clear that this was his warning.

Blaise held out his hand to me, ignoring his father. I looked down at it and back at him. What did he want me to do? Defy Garrett? Wasn't that cause for death or something? I had no idea what all the rules were, but I was sure Blaise was breaking them.

Garrett smiled at me and stepped between Blaise and me. "There are more people I'd like you to meet, Madeline. If you'll excuse us," he said, taking my hand and tucking it in his arm.

I went because it was Garrett Hughes. He was the most powerful man in this room. I had no choice.

As we walked away from them, I feared for Trev's safety.

"My oldest son is stubborn and hotheaded. He doesn't obey well, but then he never did. Don't worry about him. He'll be fine. He needs to learn a few lessons," Garrett said as we walked toward another group of people.

I tried to listen and pay attention as Garrett introduced me. I said the right things and nodded when I was supposed to. The smile on my lips I didn't feel, and the lump in my throat remained there.

This was not what I had wanted. I'd just wanted to be loved. I'd wanted Blaise. I had thought I had him. He'd said

I was the most important thing in his life. That he would die for me. But those were only words.

Words I didn't believe anymore.

Chapter TWELVE

BLAISE

The fucking rage inside of me was more intense than anything I'd ever felt. Seeing Trev's hand on Madeline had made me feel unhinged. Garrett walking around with what was mine, introducing her to people, was sending me into such a crazed madness that I wasn't sure anyone was safe.

I couldn't concentrate. All I could see was Madeline in that silver dress that showed off too much of her body. Men's eyes followed her around the room, and I despised it. She'd shown up on Trev's arm. The weak brother. To the other men in this room, that made her available.

"Blaise, are you okay? You left and didn't come back," my date for his damn thing, Helena asked. "It looked like you and your father were having words." She touched my arm.

I flinched. She couldn't touch me. Madeline had seen it, and the look in her eyes had made me physically ill. She was hurt. Garrett had brought her here so she could see this and think it was something it wasn't. He was pissed because I had refused to bring her with me. I was trying to protect her. No one needed to know where she was. That put her in danger. I needed her safe. If they thought I was with other women, they wouldn't find her.

Damn him and his fucking ego. Thinking she was safe because she was with us. That hadn't made her safe at the theater when they took her. They had hurt her. He didn't see it my way. He had said that was my mistake and that I should have told her sooner about the danger she was in. Because of me.

"Blaise?"

Helena was still there. What had she asked me? Fuck, I didn't care. She grabbed my arm again, and in the same moment, Madeline looked back over her shoulder in my direction. Her eyes immediately dropped to Helena's hand on my arm.

FUCK!

I jerked my arm free of Helena.

"This was a mistake," I said to her.

She frowned. "What was?"

I shook my head but kept my gaze locked on Madeline's back. She was so fucking stiff. I wanted to go grab her and take her out of here. Back home, and we'd never leave my goddamn room again. Just us. No fucking enemies, no damn sex traffickers, where no one could get to her. Safe with me.

"Who is she?" Helena asked casually.

She wasn't jealous because she knew full well we were not a couple. She had no desire to be a part of my world. She was also in love with a girl that her father didn't approve of. That was why I'd brought her with me. She wouldn't get any attachments.

"She's mine," I said, not taking my eyes off her.

"Looks like your daddy is trying to make you angry. I know that feeling all too well," she replied.

I didn't respond. I watched Madeline, waiting for her to need me. Right now, I knew she was hurting, and if I could kill my father, I would. He'd orchestrated this to piss me off.

"Go get her. I'll claim a headache and leave. It will be fine. Most everyone here knows we're just friends. You're not my type," she said, then nudged my arm for me to go.

I didn't look back at her, afraid if I took my eyes off Madeline, something would happen to her.

Garrett had wanted to force my hand. Well, he'd fucking won. He'd forced it with the only thing that could get to me.

Damn him.

"Thanks," I replied, still keeping my eyes locked on Madeline.

"No problem. Go remind your dad who the next boss is," she said with a teasing sound in her voice.

He didn't need reminding. This was just another one of his power plays. He knew the day was coming soon, and he also fucking knew that he had the only person I gave a shit about on his arm.

I walked up behind them and placed my hand on Madeline's back. Everyone in the group shifted their attention to me. I turned on the Hughes charm I rarely used but was there if I needed to pull it out.

"I'm sorry, but it seems my father has stolen something of mine, and I'm here to retrieve her," I told them with a smile.

I shifted my gaze to my father, holding the smile, but my eyes gave him the answers he wanted.

He nodded and released Madeline's hand. "Took you long enough. I was about to marry her off to Presley here. He is rather enamored with our girl."

"Mine. Just mine," I corrected him, feeling the pulse at my neck beating so hard that I could hear it. I slid my hand around to grip her waist, needing to hold on to her.

She was upset, and she was going to fight me. I'd had a taste of her temper enough to know what was coming next. The little flash of rebellion she'd displayed at the house before I left made me so damn hard that I was afraid to kiss her. I hadn't been certain I could kiss her, then walk away.

Dad smirked. "Very well."

I pressed Madeline's back, still not looking at her, and led her toward the back entrance leading out toward the greens. She went with me, but her body was strung so damn tight that she didn't need to say anything. I knew she was angry or nervous or both. I was going to fix it, whatever it was.

Taking her out into the night, I kept walking until I had her to the empty clubhouse. Opening the door, I gently pushed on her back to get her to go inside the dark building. She went and crossed her arms over her chest defensively when we were finally away from the view of others. Putting space between us, like she couldn't stand to be close to me. We both knew that was bullshit, but right now, she was upset.

"What are you doing?" she snapped at me.

Her gorgeous eyes were full of anger, hurt, and pain. I hated it.

"I needed you alone."

"Why? Where's your date? The one you aren't ashamed to show up with?"

Her voice cracked on the last question, and my chest felt like it might explode.

Jesus, did Garrett not understand this woman was my kryptonite? She made me so damn weak. He'd had to let her come here and make herself more of a target than she already had been to begin with. I had to protect her, and she clearly did not get that.

"You think I'm ashamed to be seen with you?" I asked her, trying to figure out where in the hell that idea had come from.

"Did you look in a motherfucking mirror before you left the house? There wasn't one heterosexual male in that goddamn building not salivating over you. And Garrett fucking knew it."

I closed the space between us, and she backed up until she hit the wall behind her.

"I don't believe you. Words mean nothing. It's actions that count. And you chose to bring someone else. I can see why. She's exotic and stunning. She belongs in your world. She's everything I'm not."

Her eyes were glistening with unshed tears, and I had never detested anyone as much as I did myself in this moment.

"Helena is beautiful, yes. But she has nothing on you. Nothing," I said, lowering my voice and touching the side of her cheek.

"I don't believe you," she said again. "You chose to bring her. Not me. And Garrett wanted me here. It was YOU who was embarrassed by me. This was not about my safety. Garrett didn't think it was dangerous."

I grabbed her waist and tugged her against me. "I was protecting you. I don't want you to be a fucking target. If my enemies see me with you, they will know that you are the one weakness that can destroy me. I didn't want another woman on my fucking arm. But I did it because you would be safe. Garrett believes the family is enough to keep you safe, but it isn't. I want you to have some chance at normalcy. Not parading you around in front of everyone was the only way I could think to do it. As for my date, I chose Helena because she'd rather lick pussy than touch a dick."

Madeline's surprised face almost made me want to laugh.

"She's … she's …"

"She's a lesbian, yes. She's a friend, and she knows how to play the part," I explained.

Madeline's arms slowly uncrossed, and she let them fall to her sides. Her gaze dropped to my chest, and I let her soak in what I should have just fucking told her to begin with. Then, she'd have been safely tucked in my house, waiting on me to get home. But after the way I had just acted in there, like a caveman beating on his chest, there was no question as to who was in my bed.

"Trev came to get me after you left. Garrett wanted me to come. I was hurt," she said, not looking up at me.

"I know," I said, sliding my hand over her hip. "He also dressed you in something he knew would turn me into a raging lunatic."

She lifted her eyes to me finally. "I didn't like her touching you. I don't care if she prefers women."

"I'd never visualized ripping my brother's arm from his body before tonight," I replied.

A soft smile touched her lips. "He was doing what he had been told to do. Don't be mad at him. I think he was secretly scared."

"He should be. He enjoyed it. Don't let that fucker fool you."

She laughed softly.

I ran my hand down over her thigh and pulled the dress up until I could get my hand inside the crotch of her panties. "Open your legs," I told her.

Her eyes went wide. "We can't do this here."

"The hell we can't," I said, shoving her legs open. "You show up in a dress that barely covers your ass and heels that make your legs look like they go on for fucking days, then, yes, baby, I'm getting a taste right here."

She inhaled sharply, causing her tits to bounce under the fabric. Slowly, she opened her legs and looked down as I slipped my entire hand down the front of her panties.

"Madeline, your pussy is already wet," I said as my fingers slid into her with ease.

"Yes," she breathed. "You were being possessive."

I grinned. "But you were mad at me when I was being possessive."

She closed her eyes tightly as I began to pump my fingers in and out of her. "My body doesn't care when I'm mad at you. Even when I thought I hated you, it didn't care."

My dick throbbed in my pants. "You're telling me this pussy got wet for me, even back when I was mean to you?"

She nodded her head.

"If I'd known that, I'd have fucked you in the damn pantry at Garrett's house and sent Trev upstairs with his snacks alone."

She let out a laugh and opened her eyes.

"Can you fuck me now?" she asked.

I'd planned on just getting her off, then tasting her, but not now. My girl wanted my dick, then she was going to get it.

I grabbed the edges of her panties and pulled them down until they fell to her ankles. "Kick them off, but leave those heels on," I told her.

She did as I'd said. I unzipped my pants and got my throbbing cock out. Picking her up, I turned and laid her down on the long boardroom table they kept in the clubhouse for meetings. She bent her knees and opened her legs. Those fucking heels right there in my face. I grabbed her foot and kissed her ankle while she watched me.

"Where's my bite mark?" I asked her, looking at her neck.

"Gina is magical with makeup," she replied, sounding breathless.

I wanted to see it, but I knew we were going back into that ballroom after this, and it would embarrass her. She'd dealt with enough tonight.

I removed my pants and boxers, then climbed over her, running my hands down her inner thighs. More men than I wanted to think about were going to jack off, thinking about taking her out of this dress tonight. But it would only be my dick getting to sink in this pussy. That gave me some comfort. Not enough. But some.

I slid in slowly, savoring it. She arched her back and pressed deeper until my balls slapped against her wetness.

"Mine," I growled, and the crazed madness I'd felt earlier when she walked in with Trev's hand on her back roared to life.

Like a wild animal, I needed to claim what was mine. Grabbing her waist, I pulled her to me and began to fuck her hard and fast.

"Oh God!" she cried as I pounded into her, wanting to make her sore. Needing her pussy to know who owned it. "BLAISE!"

"Does that hurt? I want it to hurt! I want my pussy to be fucking bruised. No man touches this. You're mine."

"Yes," she agreed and arched her back.

She liked the pain. My naughty girl was enjoying it. Fuck, she made me insane.

"FUUUCK!" I shouted, feeling my release building. "Come for me, baby. I want that pussy to soak my dick."

She screamed my name and grabbed at my legs as her body jerked with the pleasure of her orgasm. Watching her sent me over the edge, and I buried myself as deeply as I could as I shot into her, filling her with my cum. Wanting her pussy to be wet with it tonight.

When other men looked at her, I'd know my semen was between her thighs.

Chapter THIRTEEN

MADELINE

When we walked back into the house three hours later, I was exhausted. Blaise hadn't taken his hand off me all night. I'd been introduced to so many people that I would never remember all their names.

"Is Trev still alive?" Gina asked from the sofa, where she sat with a beer and a bowl of popcorn.

"Yes," Blaise replied.

"You didn't kill Garrett, did you?" she asked, frowning.

"No," he said.

"I hope someone videoed you when she walked in, looking like that, on Trev's arm," Gina said, then tossed a piece of popcorn in her mouth and grinned.

"Fuck off," he said, taking my hand and pulling me through the living room.

"Good night to you too," she called out.

We went directly to his door.

"I'm going to let you sleep for a while, but if you wake up with my face between your legs, understand that I'm feeling real fucking territorial right now. Too many men enjoyed looking at you in that damn dress tonight."

I walked past him and down the stairs while he locked the door. "My panties were wet with your cum all night. That should have made you feel better."

"It helped. It also made me fucking horny."

I laughed. When we reached the bottom of the stairs, I slipped the dress off my shoulders and let it fall to the floor before stepping out of it, and I continued to walk in nothing but my panties and heels.

"Madeline." His voice was husky.

"Hmm?" I replied, adding a slight sway to my hips.

"What are you doing?"

I reached up and pulled out the pins holding my hair up, then shook it loose.

"Getting ready for bed," I replied.

Blaise's hand grabbed the back of my panties and jerked me back against him. "That's not how you get ready for bed. That's how you get bent over and fucked."

Enjoying the fact that I could get to him so easily, I bent over and put my hands on the back of the sofa. "Don't make threats," I told him, looking back over my shoulder.

"Jesus Christ," he growled and began stripping off his tuxedo while he stared at my open legs.

I knew he could see between them. I'd left them open enough so he had a view.

The loud sound of a phone ringing interrupted us, and Blaise muttered a curse. I looked back at him as he answered his phone.

"What?" he barked out.

While he listened, he ran a hand through his hair while his teeth were clenched. "Move them in, but wait. I've got to get out of this damn tux. I'll be there in twenty. Make no move, but hold them."

He ended the call and jerked off his tuxedo jacket as his eyes met mine. "Have some mercy on me and cover yourself while I get changed. We've got an issue I have to go handle," he said as he looked at me one more time with need in his eyes, then groaned before turning to go get changed.

I grabbed the throw on the back of the sofa and wrapped it around me. He was going to do family business. I could see the hardness behind his eyes as he focused. I didn't know what he was doing, where he was going, why he had to go. All of that was foreign to me. The fear that settled inside my chest, knowing it could be dangerous, was difficult. Before, when he'd rushed off, I hadn't really dwelled on what he was doing.

I wished I could go back to that. Maybe not knowing was easier.

Blaise was pulling on a black leather jacket as he walked back out of the bathroom. I saw the flash of metal on his hip before the jacket fell into place, covering it. Swallowing hard, I lifted my eyes to meet his.

"Is it dangerous?" I asked him nervously.

The corner of his mouth lifted, but it wasn't truly a smile. "For them," he replied.

That didn't answer my question. Blaise stopped and grabbed the back of my head, then pressed a hard kiss to my lips before dropping his hand and putting distance between us.

"Get some rest. Not sure when I'll be back."

I wanted to know more. He was leaving, and the idea of him never coming back terrified me. This was his life. He didn't seem scared. He was the opposite in fact. Blaise didn't worry that he could make a wrong move and the bullet would hit him this time. Not only did he act invincible, but everyone else acted as if he were too. But Blaise wasn't Superman.

He was a human. That leather jacket did not make him bulletproof.

He didn't look back at me as he walked toward the stairs. I stood there until he was out of sight and I heard the door close upstairs. Dropping the throw, I made my way to the bathroom to get a shower and pray I could get some sleep.

Tonight had been an emotional roller coaster, and it wasn't over.

After letting the warm water wash me clean, I was slightly more relaxed. However, until Blaise was safely back, I doubted I would feel relaxed enough to sleep. I chose a pair of panties and a nightgown from the closet and then dried my hair with a towel.

My life had been so different one year ago. I'd just graduated high school. There were no plans to do anything more. I had thought Luke and Cole needed me. My life had been focused on getting by one day at a time.

My closet had consisted of four different outfits, two pairs of shoes, an old T-shirt that I'd slept in, and five pairs of white cotton panties. I'd never had much, but I hadn't been bitter about it. I had my family. I'd thought my family was something that we weren't. I had noticed things started to change with Luke and Cole, but I'd overlooked it.

Standing in the mirror now, I didn't look like the same girl. I was starting to forget her. She had been brave and determined to keep her family together. She hadn't made plans for her future. I had thought she was happy, but had she been? She hadn't known the only person who cared about her safety was a man she had never met. One who would become the most important person in her life.

Life was a funny thing. It came in waves and changed everything with finality, only to toss in something you didn't expect or prepare for, believing you were strong enough to handle it.

Chapter FOURTEEN

MADELINE

It was two days later before Blaise returned. He'd sent me a few texts, but nothing more. Gina had said this was common.

When my eyes opened this morning, I ran to the bathroom to throw up. There was no smell of bacon to trigger me. The nausea that I'd kept battling was growing worse.

I would turn twenty years old soon. I lived with a man who would one day be the boss of a wealthy, powerful crime family. My future wasn't something I was clear on, and now, I had to face the truth. I needed to take a pregnancy test. Somehow without Blaise knowing about it. I wasn't sure how that would work.

I cleaned up and dressed, then headed up to the kitchen. Gina had been busy cooking a full breakfast, and I knew then that they were returning. She had been alerted, but not me. I tried not to be hurt by that knowledge. There were too many other things going through my head. Starting with the fact that I had to get a job. I needed an income. And there was a very strong possibility I was going to be a mother.

I watched as Gina pulled out the bacon from the fridge, and I thought about going back downstairs. I should offer to help her, but I knew I couldn't smell that. If I was pregnant, I didn't want anyone to know. At least not yet. Not until I had some security. A job, a plan for the future, something to call my own.

Blaise was not going to want a baby. His life wasn't exactly baby-friendly.

Gina looked over at me and smiled, and I forced one of my own.

"Gage texted. They're headed home and hungry," she said, holding up the bacon.

I nodded and then glanced at the patio doors. "Good," I replied, thankful Blaise was safe and returning. However, getting out of this house was my main concern at the moment. "I'll come back and help, but I need some fresh air first," I explained, hoping that was enough.

She nodded. "That's fine. No need to help. I'm almost done."

Relieved, I headed for the closest door to get out of this house and the smell that I knew would trigger me.

I moved out of the backyard to make sure the smell didn't make its way out here and get to me anyway when I heard the door on the patio open. When I turned around, my eyes found Blaise walking outside with his gaze locked on me.

The smile that touched my face was genuine. I was relieved he was back and that he was safe. He was the only place I had to go for comfort even if I didn't feel as if I could tell him why I needed it. Not yet.

I stood where I was as he made his way down the steps and toward me. I fought the urge to run to him and wrap my arms around him. As I waited for him to reach me, my heart felt fluttery with excitement.

Loving Blaise Hughes was one of the hardest and most wonderful things I'd ever experienced.

When he was in arm's length, he reached out and pulled me to him. I wrapped my arms around him, and he pressed a kiss to the top of my head.

"Fuck, I missed you," he said.

My arms tightened, and I tilted my head back to look up at him. "I missed you too."

Blaise ran the pad of his thumb over my bottom lip. "I want these sweet lips on my cock, but first, we need to eat. Come inside with me."

I would go anywhere with him. He thought I was his weakness, but he had no idea just how weak he made me. Which made the future so complicated.

"Okay," I replied, knowing the smell was going to be difficult, but hoping since I'd already thrown up this morning, I'd be able to keep my nausea down.

Blaise didn't move. His gaze remained on my face as he watched me. "Something is wrong," he said, moving his hand up to cup my cheek. "Tell me."

I shrugged. "Nothing is wrong."

His eyes narrowed, and he leaned down closer to my face. "Something is fucking wrong. We'll eat, and then you can talk."

I sighed. He was too observant.

I decided to go with a partial truth. "I need a job. Even if it's working at the ranch. I need an income." Which was even truer now than it had been a week ago.

"What do you want? You have a credit card. There is no limit on it," he said, frowning.

I shook my head. "That is your money. I need to make my own. You can't pay for everything for me."

Blaise slid his hand to the back of my head, tangling his fingers in my hair. "I take care of you."

"But you shouldn't financially. I can't let you keep doing that."

He scowled. "We'll talk about this after breakfast."

This was going to be a fight. He'd just gotten back, and I didn't want to fight. But he'd pushed me to tell him what was wrong, and this was better than telling him there was a chance I could be pregnant.

His hand grabbed mine, and he started toward the house. I went willingly, silently praying I didn't vomit at the smells when the door opened. I inhaled slowly and then sighed in relief. Blaise kept my hand in his as we walked into the kitchen. The others were already around the table with their plates piled high.

Gage held up a hand and saluted me, then stuck a forkful of pancakes in his mouth. Huck nodded his head my way in greeting. Levi was too busy cramming his mouth with scrambled eggs to care who had entered.

Had they eaten since they'd been gone? They looked like ravenous wolves.

"What do you want?" Blaise asked me.

I glanced over to see Gina setting his plate of food at the table.

"I'll go fix mine," I told him.

His hand tightened on mine. "Not today," he said.

"I'll get you some of everything," Gina told me.

I looked over at her and hated to know she was making my plate after cooking all of this alone. "I can do it," I said.

"No." Blaise's voice was hard. "Not leaving my side."

I sighed, and Gina winked at me. "I got it."

We were going to have to discuss this later too.

"No bacon," I told her then.

When I turned back to the table, I saw Huck studying me with a frown. Dang Huck and his nosy self.

"Angel," Gina said with surprise.

Blaise stiffened beside me.

"I didn't expect you to join us. Come here and tell me what you want to eat," Gina told her.

Blaise let go of my hand and took a biscuit from his plate, then handed it to me. "Eat this." It sounded more like a command than a request.

I took it and didn't argue. He was tense because Angel was in the room and we were together.

"Should I leave?" I whispered. "Or move to the other side of the table?"

He shook his head. "No."

Okay then. This wasn't awkward at all. I could feel the others glancing over at me, and I knew they were wondering what was going to happen.

"You can sit on the other side of Blaise," Gina told her.

I glanced up from the biscuit I'd taken a small bite of to see Angel's eyes locked on Blaise.

"You were gone." She said it so softly that I barely heard her.

"Work, Angel," Blaise said to her, but his voice was gentle.

She shifted her eyes from him to me quickly. "She came back," Angel whispered, but her gaze was locked on me now.

I felt Blaise's hand slide over the top of my leg and squeeze. "Yes, she did," he replied.

Angel's eyes darted back to Blaise, but she said nothing else.

"Eat, Angel," Blaise instructed her, but his voice wasn't hard or commanding.

I didn't want to be jealous of the gentle way he spoke to her. He had to speak to her that way. If he spoke to her harshly, then I doubted she could handle it.

She reminded me of a beautiful porcelain doll. If she hadn't been shot, would Blaise have ever come looking for me?

Would he have ever loved me? I dropped my eyes back to the biscuit and mentally scolded myself for letting my thoughts go there. Those were pointless and made me sound shallow and self-centered.

A plate was placed in front of me then, and I lifted my gaze up to Gina. "Thank you," I said, and she flashed me an apologetic smile.

This awkwardness was going to have to stop when Angel was in the room. It wasn't fair to her. This was her home. I had to find a way to make it work.

"Damn, you can cook, woman," Levi said as he reached for his coffee. "I was fucking starving."

"You ate three chocolate bars and had a bag of chips three hours ago," Huck pointed out.

Levi shrugged. "Those were snacks. We've not had real food in days."

I wondered where they had been, but I didn't ask. I knew by now that wasn't something we discussed.

"Eat," Blaise said to me, and I lifted my eyes to meet his. "You need some energy."

I frowned. "What for?"

He smirked, then raised his eyebrows.

Oh.

I picked up the fork and cut into my pancakes, then put a bite into my mouth. Blaise's hand remained on my thigh as he ate. He spoke to Angel a few times, and I couldn't hear her whispered reply over Gage's voice, saying he was planning to go somewhere called Devil's Lair later today. He wanted Huck and Levi to go with him, but he never mentioned Blaise.

Gina pulled out the chair at the end of the table closest to me and sat down with her cup of coffee. "I was thinking that we should get out of the house today. Boys are back, and the nurse will be here soon to stay with Angel. We could go shopping," she said to me, looking hopeful.

"No," Blaise replied before I could even open my mouth.

Gina didn't argue, but I turned my head to look at him.

"I can't stay in this house forever."

His jaw flexed. "I know. I'll take you somewhere today. Wherever you want to go."

I liked the idea of going somewhere with Blaise much better, but I felt bad for Gina. Did she have friends? Or was her life always taking care of Angel?

"Gina could come too," I said.

Blaise narrowed his eyes at me. He didn't want anyone going with us. That was clear.

"Gina has friends. She can do something with them. We need to go to the ranch. Look into getting you set up in the office again."

He was going to let me work? Without a fight?

A smile crossed my face. I was relieved that he was giving in to it without being difficult.

"Really?" I wanted to grab his face and kiss it.

A grin tugged on his lips. "Yes."

I started to say something, but a loud clatter interrupted me, and Blaise moved back, quickly jerking around to see what had happened.

Angel was standing up, and her plate was on the floor, shattered. Then, she began to scream. Blaise shot up and reached for her, and she clung to him. My heart was racing as I watched the scene. No one else was speaking, but all eyes were on them.

Gina walked around me and went to Angel. "That's all for this morning, sis. If you can't control yourself, then no breakfast down here," she said to Angel.

When Gina reached for her, Angel batted her hand away and held on to Blaise. He and Gina exchanged a silent look, and then he took Angel's arms from around him and wrapped an arm around her shoulders.

"I'll go with you," he said.

Angel visibly relaxed, and they walked out of the kitchen. My chest felt tight, and I wasn't sure how I was supposed to handle this or feel about it. Angel needed him. That was clear. She felt as if he belonged to her, and she didn't like sharing. How was I going to get her to accept me?

"Sorry about that," Gina said as she came back with a broom in her hand.

"It's okay. I just don't know what I can do to make her feel okay with me," I said, turning back to my plate of food.

"Shit, that ain't gonna happen. You're the first female she's had to see him with. Blaise never brought women here. Angel isn't used to him touching another woman," Gage drawled, leaning back in his chair, his eyes on me.

That wasn't promising.

"Shut up," Huck said to him.

Gage shrugged. "What? She lives here. She needs to know. Hell, she's family. Time she gets to hear all the shit."

Thank you, Gage.

I agreed. If this was to be my life, then, yes, I needed to know what was going on around me.

"Blaise tells her all the shit. Not you." Huck's tone held a clear warning.

"Listen, he's going to be up there awhile. She's missed him, and that's her way of demanding his attention. Want to go watch the new season of *Yellowstone* with me?" Gina asked as she finished cleaning up the mess Angel had made.

The truth was, I didn't want to watch anything, but I also didn't want to go downstairs by myself for however long he was with her.

I nodded and stood up, then took my plate. "I'll clean up the kitchen. You cooked," I told her.

"You sure?" Gina asked me.

Huck cleared his throat loudly, and I looked at him. He was focused on Gina when he shook his head. Aggravated by this entire situation. I glared at him.

"Listen, Huck. If I want to clean this kitchen, then I am damn well gonna clean it. Stop telling people what to do where I'm concerned. I don't belong to you." My voice rose as I spoke until I was close to yelling.

His eyes widened, and I heard Gage chuckle. Spinning around, I went to the sink and decided I would ignore them all. Except Gina.

"Let me help," she said, coming up beside me.

She wasn't their damn maid.

I shook my head. "I refuse to let you clean after you cooked and served everyone. Go start your show, and I'll be in there when I'm done."

A smile touched her lips, and she shrugged. "Okay."

Chapter FIFTEEN

BLAISE

Garrett was getting what he wanted. Simply because I couldn't tell her no. She wanted a job, and this was all I could allow without losing my fucking mind, worrying about her. Garrett wanted Madeline as tied into the family as she could get. He was doing it for Eli, and I understood that. Eli would fucking love knowing his granddaughter was here. Working within the family.

She was right. I couldn't keep her in the house, and she couldn't go everywhere with me. There was shit she could never be a part of.

This morning, having Angel in the kitchen and then dealing with one of her fits hadn't sat well with me. Once, it had made sense for Angel to live in my house, but I didn't see how this was going to continue to work. Not with Madeline living there, and Madeline would be staying.

Now that we were at the ranch, I stood back and watched as Deidra showed Madeline the things that had changed since she'd been gone the past few weeks.

Deidra had worked for my father most of my life. She was older than him, and he moved her around in different areas when needed. He'd put her in this position until Madeline's return. I knew he hadn't planned on allowing her to be gone long. If she hadn't come back with me, Garrett would have stepped in.

Things weren't perfect, and we had shit to figure out, like the fact that she thought she needed money to live. I'd let her work, but I'd be damned if she spent her money on things she needed. She was mine, and I'd take care of her. What the fuck she thought she needed money for, I didn't know.

"Maddy!" Trev's voice called out from behind me.

I glared over my shoulder as my brother came walking into the office.

Trev gave me his smug, bright smile, then looked back at Madeline. "You're back." He clapped his hands together.

She smiled at him, and I fucking hated it. That smile was mine.

"I can see you are broken up about my leaving," Deidra said to him teasingly.

Trev put his hand on his heart. "Oh, I'll miss your beautiful face, Dee. But I'm sure you'll be around."

Deidra let out a bark of laughter. "You're full of shit. My feelings aren't hurt. I have eyes. I understand. You boys like the eye candy, and this one is beautiful."

"Not his to look at," I said.

Deidra cut her eyes at me, then smiled. "Eli sure would love to know his baby girl's daughter was here. Where she belongs."

Madeline's gaze moved to meet mine. There were so many insecurities inside those blue eyes. Why? What more could I do to reassure her that she was all I wanted? Why did she look so damn haunted? Like at any moment, I was going to change my mind and walk away?

"She's home now," I agreed, keeping my eyes on Madeline's.

There was a spark of hope there. It wasn't what I wanted to see. I wanted to see her look at me with the assurance that she knew she was home.

"Literally? Because if she's moving in here, then I'm going to request she gets the room next to mine," Trev said.

He was trying to piss me off.

"Go," I growled.

Trev threw out his hands like he was confused. "What did I do?"

"NOW!" I ordered.

I saw the grin on his face when he looked back at Madeline and winked. If I thought the fucker was serious for one second, I'd break one or more of his bones. He knew the ranks, and he knew Madeline was mine.

"Play nice," Madeline scolded him, still grinning.

Damn, why did she have to smile at him like that?

He bowed to her, then saluted me before backing out of the office.

"That boy is a handful," Deidra said. "He's got Garrett's charm with none of the edge."

Or black soul. Trev might be redeemable, but eventually, he'd have to face the truth of the family. When that day came and he had to be Garrett Hughes's son in the face of hell, then he'd change. He wouldn't be carefree and spoiled forever.

"Now, if you have any questions, contact me. This is my number. I'll be available at any time," Deidra assured Madeline.

Madeline thanked her, and when Deidra finally left, I closed the office door.

"No. Not in here. This is my job," Madeline said, her eyes big as she watched me moving toward her.

"What? I wasn't going to do anything. Just wanted my girl alone for a few minutes," I said, coming behind the desk.

Madeline moved back away from me, and a laugh rumbled in my chest. Damn, she was cute. She held up her hands in front of her.

"Blaise, there could be cameras in here," she whispered.

I nodded. There were three. I pointed to the corner behind her, over the door, and then to the front of the office desk. Madeline's eyes darted to each place, then back at me.

"Why are you still coming at me then?" she asked nervously. "I need to work."

I shrugged as I watched her. Seeing her licking her lips, nervous, turned me on, but she was safe. Those cameras were watched all day by security. I wasn't about to let some other man see Madeline when she was worked up. That was for my eyes only.

"I wanted a kiss before I left," I told her truthfully.

She narrowed her eyes. "Promise that's all?"

I nodded. "Swear."

She stopped moving away from me and planted her hands on her hips. "Be good," she warned me.

I reached out and grabbed the loops on her jeans, then pulled her to me. "I'm always good."

She laughed then. The only other sound I loved better than that was when she was crying out my name while she orgasmed.

"You, Blaise Hughes, are rarely good."

I brushed my lips against hers, then whispered, "I make you feel good."

She sighed and leaned into me then. "Yes, you do."

I started to cover her mouth when the office door opened. Madeline tensed, and I glared back over my shoulder to find my father walking inside.

"You don't want to give the security team a show," he said.

"I wasn't going to," I replied angrily.

Madeline was stepping back from me. I hadn't been ready to let her go yet. *Damn Garrett.*

"Let Madeline get to work, and you come with me up to the house. We have a meeting to attend," he told me, then walked past me toward Madeline. "Glad you're back. Wasn't the same without you."

She smiled at him nervously. It was clear he terrified her, and I wished she understood how unnecessary that was. Garrett would die to protect her. We all would.

"Thank you for letting me come back," she said.

Garrett beamed at her. "Letting you? Hell, it was your job. Deidra was just holding down the fort until you returned. I'll take this distraction away. When you get ready for lunch, go on up to the house and eat what Ms. Jimmie has prepared in there. No need for you to have to eat with the hands in the dining hall down here."

"Okay, I will," she agreed.

Garrett started to leave, and his eyes locked on mine. "Work to do," he said simply.

I shifted my gaze to Madeline. "I'll come back later," I said before following Garrett out of the room.

Chapter SIXTEEN

MADELINE

The last two mornings, when I'd woken up sick, Blaise was already awake and upstairs. I'd been trying to focus on working again and pretending there wasn't another issue I had to handle.

Today, however, I had decided that I would get a pregnancy test. I wasn't sure how I would get it or who I could confide in to help me get it. I did have a car now, but Blaise always took me to work and picked me up. Waiting until he was gone again could be days or weeks. I never knew.

Angel had been absent in the mornings since the plate-smashing incident. While I was taking my time eating the avocado toast that I'd made myself, trying to come up with a reason to drive to work today that Blaise wouldn't question, Angel's screaming rang through the house.

Blaise had been talking to Huck about the first race of the season, which was two months away, when she did it. He stood up without a word and left the room to go see what was wrong. Huck drank his coffee and peered at me over his cup.

"How you handling that?" he asked me.

I knew by *that*, he meant Blaise having to go running when Angel had an episode, I shrugged. I was handling it. Not being here all day and feeling like my presence was keeping her confined upstairs helped things. I didn't feel in the way as much.

"You gonna snap over it eventually?" he asked me.

Snap over it? I shook my head. "No ..." I trailed off.

He took a drink, then set his cup down. "You're a woman. You don't think you're gonna get jealous, sharing your man?"

I didn't see it that way. It wasn't as if he were sleeping with Angel. She just had emotional trauma, and he soothed her.

"That would make me a bitch," I replied honestly.

He smirked, but said nothing more.

I finished my breakfast in silence, and when it was time for me to go and Blaise hadn't returned, I realized I'd been given my break. I would have to drive myself today. I didn't ask Huck. Getting permission would likely lead to someone else driving me. Blaise had bought me that car because he said I needed one. I hadn't driven it yet. Now was the one time it was going to come in handy.

I'd placed the keys in my purse, and my own cash was also safely tucked inside. I cleaned my plate and cup, then wrote a quick note to Blaise and left it on the counter.

Huck wasn't around anywhere, so I took that as my time to escape. Just as I reached the door leading to the garage, I heard Angel scream out again. Blaise wasn't going to be free anytime soon. Closing the door behind me quietly, I went down the row of cars until I found the silver Mercedes that Blaise had refused to return.

I climbed inside, and it took a few minutes longer than I would have liked to figure out where everything was located in order to drive this thing.

No one had come looking for me by the time I opened the garage door and backed out. Feeling accomplished, I made it down the driveway, and the gate swung open when I got close enough, making it all the easier to leave.

If I was late for work and Blaise was alerted, then he'd panic. I decided that I would slip out to the closest pharmacy and get the test I needed on my lunch break.

I was on the road for less than ten minutes when my phone rang. I winced, knowing only one person ever called me. The screen on the dashboard lit up and asked me if I wanted to answer the call.

I replied, "Yes," wondering if that was all I had to do.

"Madeline." Blaise's voice came through the speakers on the car, and it was clear that he was pissed.

"Yes," I replied.

"Where are you?"

"On my way to work in the car you bought me that I never drive," I replied as sweetly as I could.

He sighed deeply and didn't reply right away.

"You were busy, and I didn't want to disturb things," I added.

He muttered a curse. "Are you going straight there?" he finally asked.

"Yes!"

He was silent another moment. Then, "I'm sorry."

"It's okay. I can drive. Angel needed you," I assured him.

"You come first," he replied sharply.

I didn't want to test that, but it was sweet that he had said it.

"I am fine," I replied.

But how long would my being there with her be fine? When was he going to decide that it was too much on Angel? He would grow weary of her fits, and the only way to stop it was for me not to be there. Not an issue I was going to tackle right now. I needed to stay focused on one thing at a time.

"Did you finish your food?" he asked me.

Smiling at his concern, I replied, "Yes, I did. Did you?"

"No. Lost my fucking appetite when I saw your note," he said.

Maybe I should have told him I was leaving. I felt guilty now.

"Go eat. Please," I said to him.

He grunted, but said nothing.

"Independence is good for me," I told him. I didn't need to rely on him for everything.

"I want you to need me," he said.

"Oh, I do. Regularly," I assured him.

I heard Huck's voice in the background.

"Call me when you get there. I've got something we have to go see about. I'll stop by the ranch when I'm done."

"Okay. Be safe," I told him.

"Call me," he repeated, and then the call ended.

"Well, goodbye to you too," I muttered to no one.

Chapter SEVENTEEN

BLAISE

Although the pictures of Etta did look almost exactly like Madeline, I could see her in *his* face too. The son of a bitch didn't know I had been tracking him for months. I was concerned that he'd been behind her abduction at the movie theater. Word had gotten out about Madeline, and anyone who had known Etta would know she was Eli's granddaughter.

Liam Walsh stood in ripped jeans and black combat boots, his Glock on his hip and his arms crossed over his chest as he spoke to the men with him. The cigarette between his lips hung loosely. From what I'd found on the man, he had cleaned up somewhat with age. There had been a riot within their organization fifteen years ago, and his father had been killed, along with several others. He had disappeared after that.

Garrett had to know this, but he'd never felt the need to share it with me. Liam, along with a few of the guys he'd grown up with, had formed a biker club. They owned several strip clubs in Miami, had call girls they hired out to deep pockets, and ran a porn ring, where they filmed and uploaded to a private website that charged via monthly subscriptions. Seemed he had left the drugs behind and moved into the sex market only.

He scanned the area, but I was hidden from his sight. A girl came walking out of the back entrance of the club he was currently at, wearing red stiletto heels and a dress that barely covered her snatch. The fake tits were only covered by a thin strip down the middle of each one, just barely keeping the nipples from view.

"Dayum," Gage's voice drawled through the piece in my ear.

He was across the lot in his own spot, as were Levi and Huck. We had the area surrounded to keep our asses covered.

Liam slid his hand up the back of her dress, and she squealed. He then slapped her ass and crossed his arms over his chest again. They were moving here, to Ocala. The Devil's Lair had been sold, and from the intel I'd gotten on it, Liam Walsh had bought it in cash.

He was coming closer because of Madeline. I was fucking sure of it. My hands fisted, and I inhaled sharply. I could put a bullet in his head from here. This shit would end. Madeline wouldn't have any more hell in her life.

But if she ever found out I'd killed her real father, would she forgive that? FUCK! How was I supposed to protect her if I couldn't kill the motherfuckers who could hurt her?

"Not the right time." Huck's voice came through the earpiece. He always knew what I was thinking.

He was right. I had to know more. Right now, I wasn't one hundred percent positive that he had been behind Madeline's abduction. From what I'd learned, the fucker was well liked. He had made important connections by selling high-end pussy to powerful men. That was why they liked him.

He smiled then at something one of the other men had said. My gut clenched. There was something about it that looked like Madeline's smile. God, I hated this. Not knowing and needing to keep her safe.

My phone vibrated in my pocket, and I pulled it out to see an alert that Madeline was moving. She was driving. Where the fuck was she going? It was lunchtime. She shouldn't be leaving the ranch yet.

"Pull back for now," I said to the others, then headed back to the truck.

Something was off. As soon as I was back inside the truck, I dialed her number, but she didn't answer. Slamming my hand on the steering wheel, I backed out and looked at the tracker to see where she was heading. Huck would need to ride back with Gage and Levi. I had to go make sure Madeline was safe.

Chapter EIGHTEEN

MADELINE

The test was tucked in my purse as I pulled back onto the road and headed back to the ranch. I had successfully gotten in and out of the pharmacy in less than five minutes. No one would notice my absence. Turning onto the road that led down past Moses Mile and then to the Hughes Farm, I finally relaxed.

Blaise had called me when I was leaving the pharmacy and I'd ignored it. I could just tell him I'd left my phone in the office and had to go get lunch at the house.

I hated the idea of lying to him, but right now, there was no other option. Except to tell him the truth, and that idea made me sick. He was the one who had gotten me on the shot. He didn't want to chance getting me pregnant. If I was though and the shot hadn't protected me from it, then what? I would have no choice but to tell him.

"Please let it be negative," I whispered.

I didn't know who I was talking to because I'd given up praying to God when I was a kid. He had never answered my prayers, and eventually, I tired of it. I had grown up.

The big, arched entrance to Hughes Farm greeted me as I pulled in and went to park exactly where I had this morning. Grabbing my purse, I headed for the office, glancing around only for a moment to make sure I hadn't been seen. I needed to take this test before I went back to the house today. I didn't want to toss it in the trash there, where it could be found. If I'd had time, I would have taken it at the pharmacy and tossed it away there, but I'd been in a hurry.

My office door was open, and thankfully, the room was empty when I rushed inside and closed the door behind me. I needed a moment to calm down again. My adrenaline was pumping. There was a bathroom attached to the office, and I knew I'd have my privacy. Plus, I had several more hours of work. Plenty of time.

Sinking down into the black leather chair, I looked down at the paperwork in front of me just as the door to the office swung open. Blaise came walking inside, his gaze locked on me. He looked like a man on a mission, as if he knew I was keeping something from him and he intended to figure out exactly what it was.

"Blaise," I said breathlessly. He'd startled me.

He cocked one eyebrow, but said nothing.

I waited, and silence remained as he studied me.

Finally uncomfortable with his not speaking, I cleared my throat. "Uh, are you here for a reason?" I asked.

He narrowed his eyes and tilted his head to the side. He continued to look at me as if he could find the answers to his questions on my face. That was when I realized he knew I'd been gone.

Had he come here before I returned and parked somewhere I couldn't see his truck? Oh crap, had he called me when he arrived and I was gone?

"I called you," he said slowly.

I swallowed nervously. "Oh, you did?" I reached for my phone in my pocket. "It must be on silent."

I'd decided not to lie and say I'd gone to lunch. He knew something. I just wasn't sure how much he knew.

Blaise walked around the desk until he was on my side. Our eyes locked.

"Madeline, do you honestly think that I'd give you a vehicle to drive and not put a tracking device on it after someone took you from me once already?"

I felt as the blood drained from my face. There was a tracker on my car. I had known that, but I'd assumed he wouldn't be checking that constantly since he knew I was at work.

"My phone has a tracker already," I pointed out. I did know that.

"Yes, but it's different. It doesn't send me alerts when your car is moving."

Well, shit. I let out a sigh and crossed my arms over my chest, suddenly annoyed. Did I have no privacy at all? It felt like every move I made was watched closely. It was a miracle I could go to the toilet alone.

"Tell me, Blaise, why do you need alerts when the car you claim is mine—but isn't mine at all—starts moving? How is that keeping me safe? Do you think a kidnapper is going to use that car to take me? No. They wouldn't be that dumb. The tracker on my car must only be so that you know what I'm doing and where I am at all times. You have a trust issue."

Blaise put his hands on the armrests of my chair, caging me in. "I need to know you are safe when you're driving alone. You're mine, and because of that, you're a fucking target."

That excuse made me angry. He used it too much. Whenever he wanted me to understand his reasoning behind things. Always my safety and me being a target.

"I was unaware I needed permission to go buy aspirin for a headache. I've been alerted now, and I will be sure it doesn't happen again!" I shouted in his face.

"Jimmie would have given you aspirin when you went to get lunch. She has all the pain meds you need. What is hurting you?" he replied.

I shoved him back, using both my hands, and stood up. I didn't like feeling as if he had all the control. I might be keeping something from him, but I still had a point. He didn't own me. I should have my freedom.

"Why can't I go to a store if I want to? Why must I ask permission? I'm not a child. You aren't my daddy."

Blaise smirked then, and my hand suddenly itched to slap his gorgeous face.

"I'm about to put you over my lap and spank your ass," he warned in a low voice.

I pointed at the cameras. "Uh, no," I replied and went to walk away from him.

His hand wrapped around my arm and pulled me back against his chest. He was quicker than I was. Damn him. I could feel his erection against my back.

"That bathroom doesn't have cameras. You keep pushing me with that smart mouth, and we will forgo the spanking. I'll shove my cock in that mouth."

I closed my eyes tightly, angry that his words turned me on. I needed help. I was as crazy as he was, and it just seemed to be getting worse. He had tracked me and come here to grill me about where I had been. That was not okay. I had to remember that.

"I have work to do, Blaise," I said through clenched teeth.

I would not think about his dick. I would not. I would not.

He ran his hands down my arms, then let me go. "Okay. Work then," he said and stepped back. "But please let me know when you're going somewhere alone. I don't know who is watching you. My guys haven't seen anything recently, but that's just been since you left town. Word is going to get out that you're back now because of the gala."

The gentle pleading in his voice got to me. He was worried about me. Apparently, he had good reason to be.

If he didn't care about me, then I'd be alone. As much as I loved Blaise, I knew I needed him too. He was all I had in this world.

Chapter NINETEEN

MADELINE

The two blue lines were said to change your life. How much more could mine be changed? Yet here I was, about to have it all change again. With paper towels, I wrapped up the proof that my nausea was a pregnancy symptom, then tucked it under other garbage in the can.

I couldn't go to the pharmacy alone for safety reasons, and I was bringing a child into this world. This was not a life you raised a child in, and Blaise was not a father figure. What kind of mom would I be when I barely remembered mine? I had no model to follow. I'd had no mother to teach me how to do it right. I couldn't do this to a child. It wasn't about not being ready. It was about the life it would be given. With a mother who had no clue how to be a mother.

"Hey, you okay?"

Saxon's voice startled me, and I lifted my head from my hands and looked up at him. He was standing just inside my office door with concern on his face. Once, I'd thought I could talk to him, but I knew I couldn't now. He was loyal to the family. To Blaise. I was beginning to understand that, but it still felt as if I had no real friends. They were all conditional on Blaise.

"Yeah, just tired." I managed to smile.

Saxon didn't look convinced. He walked farther into the room. "You sure?"

I wanted to laugh. Even if I wanted to tell him my problem, there were cameras all around this room.

I nodded. "Positive. How's life at Moses Mile? I heard y'all bought a new thoroughbred that's already being talked about in the racing world. That's exciting."

The closer we got to fall, the more the world of racing was on everyone's mind and in their conversations. Garrett had seemed concerned about Moses Mile's newest addition. He didn't like to lose, but then what man did? It was odd to me the way they competed in racing horses. The Houstons' seemed to always do what Garrett told them to do. Maybe it was part of the racing world that I didn't understand.

"Yeah, he cost more than Dad wanted to spend, but I think he'll pay off in the long run. How're the riding lessons going?"

There had been no riding lessons lately. Blaise seemed preoccupied with family business.

I shrugged. "They're not. No time," I replied.

Saxon continued to study me, and it made me uncomfortable. I knew he couldn't look at my face and tell that I was pregnant, but I still didn't want him looking at me so closely.

Standing up, I reached for my purse. "It's about time I head back to the house," I told him, although I wasn't leaving without letting Blaise know. Fighting with him over my driving was not something I wanted to do again today.

"I saw your wheels out there." He looked guilty then.

Yes, Saxon, you lied to me.

I raised my eyebrows and nodded.

He pressed his lips together, then looked off with a small chuckle. "Sorry about all that," he said as his gaze shifted back to me. "You know I only did what I thought was best for you. I wanted you safe too."

And you are scared of Blaise. I didn't add that though. I kept it silent. We both knew that was the underlying truth.

I shrugged. "It's fine. I get it," I assured him.

He looked like he was about to say more when Blaise walked up behind him. My eyes lifted to meet his over Saxon's shoulder. He looked at Saxon, then to me.

"Sax," he said simply, and Saxon turned around to face Blaise.

"Hey, Blaise," he replied.

Blaise looked past him toward me. "You ready?"

I turned off the computer and stepped around the desk. Seeing him made me feel better even if I was keeping a secret that I didn't know how to tell him. It always felt like he could fix everything.

"You headed up to the house?" Blaise asked Saxon.

He nodded. "Yeah, going to the springs with Trev and others."

Blaise pulled something out of his back pocket and handed it to him. "Give this to Garrett."

Saxon took it, and all I could see was a white envelope. He nodded, then turned back to me. "Bye, Maddy," he said.

"Bye," I replied and watched him go.

Blaise held out his hand to me. "Let's go home."

Home. He felt like home, but his house did not. It was a strange situation. Again, another thing that wasn't good for a baby. How would I bring a baby into that house? Angel wouldn't handle it well. Her screams and tantrums would get worse.

"I'm not driving you if that is why you're frowning. I'm following you. That's all," he said to me as he took my hand and pulled me close to him.

I managed to smile. "Okay."

Blaise lowered his head and pressed a kiss to my lips. "You look tired," he whispered as his mouth hovered over mine.

I nodded.

The sound of his phone ringing ended his close study of me. He straightened and pulled it out of his pocket. "Yeah," he replied, not caring that he sounded annoyed.

He stilled a moment before looking back at me. The frown line between his brows was never a good sign. He didn't say anything else but continued to listen, then ended the call. His steady gaze on me made me nervous. I felt like he was reading all my thoughts.

Finally, he slipped his phone back into his pocket, and his fingers threaded through mine before he began walking to the exit of the stables. The silence was not comforting. With Blaise, it never was. I could hear my heartbeat in my ears; it was thumping so hard. I wished he would say something. Anything.

When we stepped out into the sunlight, he headed to his truck, not letting go of my hand. My SUV was in the other direction. I started to say something, but his body language made me stay silent.

Once we were at his truck, he opened the passenger door, and then, without an explanation, he picked me up and sat me in the seat before closing the door and walking over to the driver's side. I took a deep breath, trying to calm my nerves. I shouldn't let him get to me like this. It wasn't like he was going to hurt me. The man had never hurt me. He wouldn't even let me go do small errands alone, for fear someone else would hurt me.

Blaise opened his door and climbed in, not looking at me as he started the engine. I didn't want to continue this entire ride in silence.

"Are you going to tell me why I'm in your truck and not driving my own home?" I asked him.

He glanced at me then, and his eyes dropped to my stomach, then lifted to meet my gaze. "Are you going to tell me what you really bought at the pharmacy today?" he replied.

Shit. He knew. How did he know? Did they have cameras there he could get ahold of too?

My hands fisted in my lap, and I looked away from him.

"It wasn't motherfucking aspirin," he told me.

"No, it wasn't. But you already know, don't you, Blaise? So, why ask me?" I said angrily.

This was not how I'd wanted to tell him. I'd needed time to deal with it myself. But he had eyes everywhere. It was as frustrating as it was infuriating.

He pulled over just as we drove out of the entrance and put the truck in park.

"Why wouldn't you tell me the truth, Madeline?" he asked me.

I felt his eyes on me as I sat there, staring down at my fisted hands.

"I was scared. I am scared," I admitted.

"Look at me," he ordered.

I lifted my head and turned my gaze to him.

"Scared of me?" he asked.

I shook my head. "No. Scared of the reality. What it would mean," I choked out, feeling emotion clogging my throat.

"You're mine," he said.

"For now," I whispered.

He narrowed his gaze. "What the fuck does that mean?"

The lump in my throat was making it hard to swallow. I had to force it down. I didn't want to cry. Not now.

"What happens when you don't want me anymore? What happens when it's not just me and there is … there's a baby? Then, we can't have sex anywhere and anytime we want. We will have diapers to change and a baby who needs attention. I will be a mother. I won't be so easily accessible, and I'll have someone else who needs me."

"Fuck!" Blaise growled out, then swung open his door and got out.

I blinked back the tears, feeling as if I might shatter into a million pieces. Taking several deep breaths, I watched as he walked around the front of the truck until he was jerking my door open.

"What—" I started to ask him, but he was picking me up and getting me out before I could finish my question.

Blaise put my feet on the ground in front of him, then let go of my waist to cup my face instead. "I'm going to make something real fucking clear, Madeline. I thought I already had, but I guess it wasn't clear enough," he said as he looked down at me. "I'd never loved anyone. It wasn't something I was raised to do. I didn't need love. I thought it made a man weak. But I fell in love with YOU.

"Before I spoke to you and held you the first time, I would have taken a motherfucking bullet for you. Standing back and watching you be strong, brave, and so innocent in the midst of the shit life you had been handed was so damn hard. But you survived. I respected that. You were loyal. I wanted that. You loved without question. I fucking needed that. My need to keep you safe pushed me to keep you from me. I tried to protect you from this life. From danger. From all your mother had fled from. But I couldn't. Because I needed you more than I needed my next breath. So, baby, when I say that you're mine, that isn't just your hot little pussy. That's all of you. Because I want it all. Not for now. Forever."

The tears I had fought so hard not to shed were running freely when he finished. Why he had chosen me I didn't understand, but then I realized he saw me differently than I saw myself. I wanted to see me the way he did. Maybe then I wouldn't be so insecure.

"Madeline, are you pregnant?" he asked me, holding my gaze.

"Yes," I whispered.

He wrapped his arms around me and pulled me to his chest. I buried my face and let out a sob. It was a relief to cry. His arms tightened around me, and I was home. Safe. He made everything better.

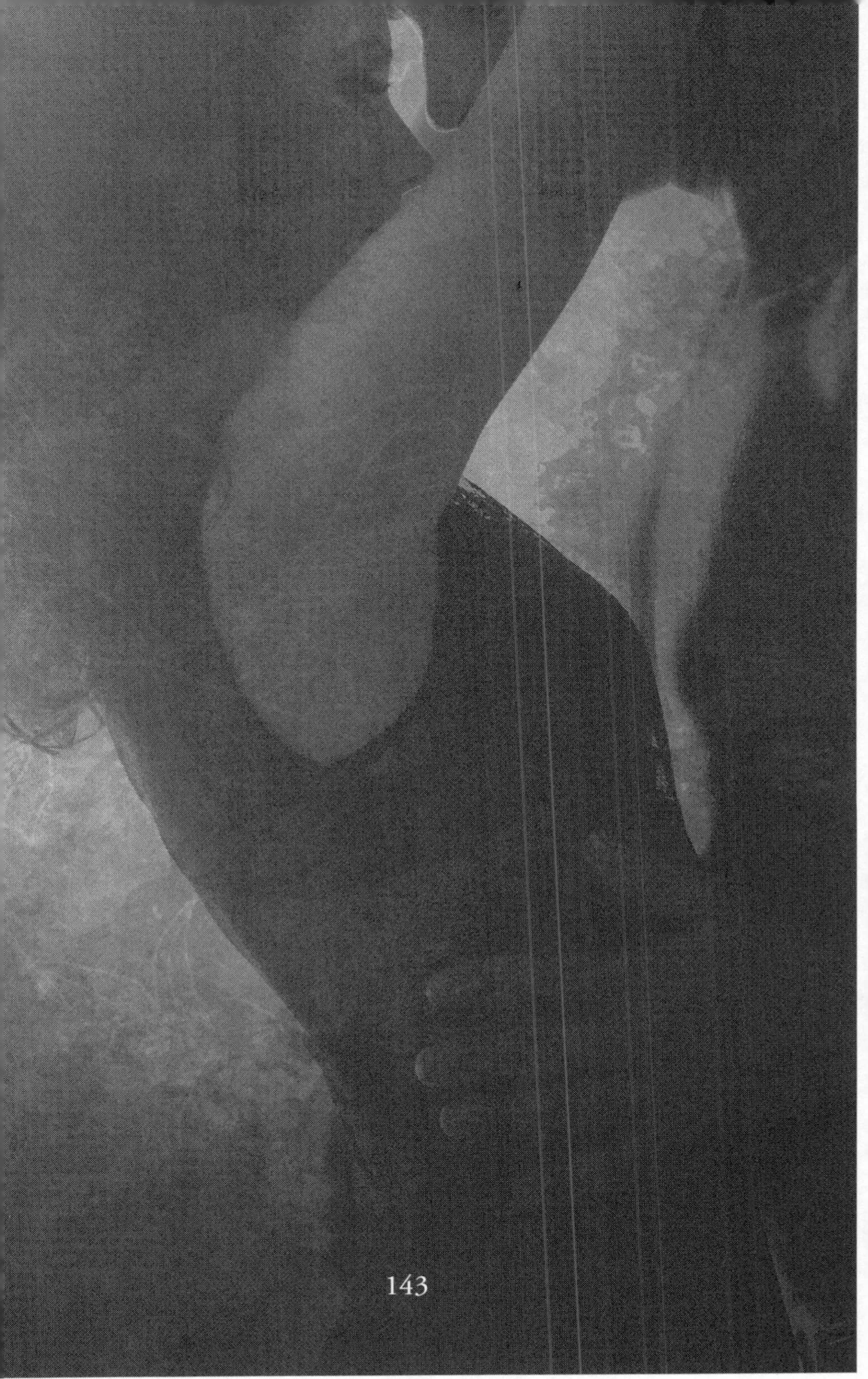

II

"We know what we are, but know not what we may be."

—William Shakespeare

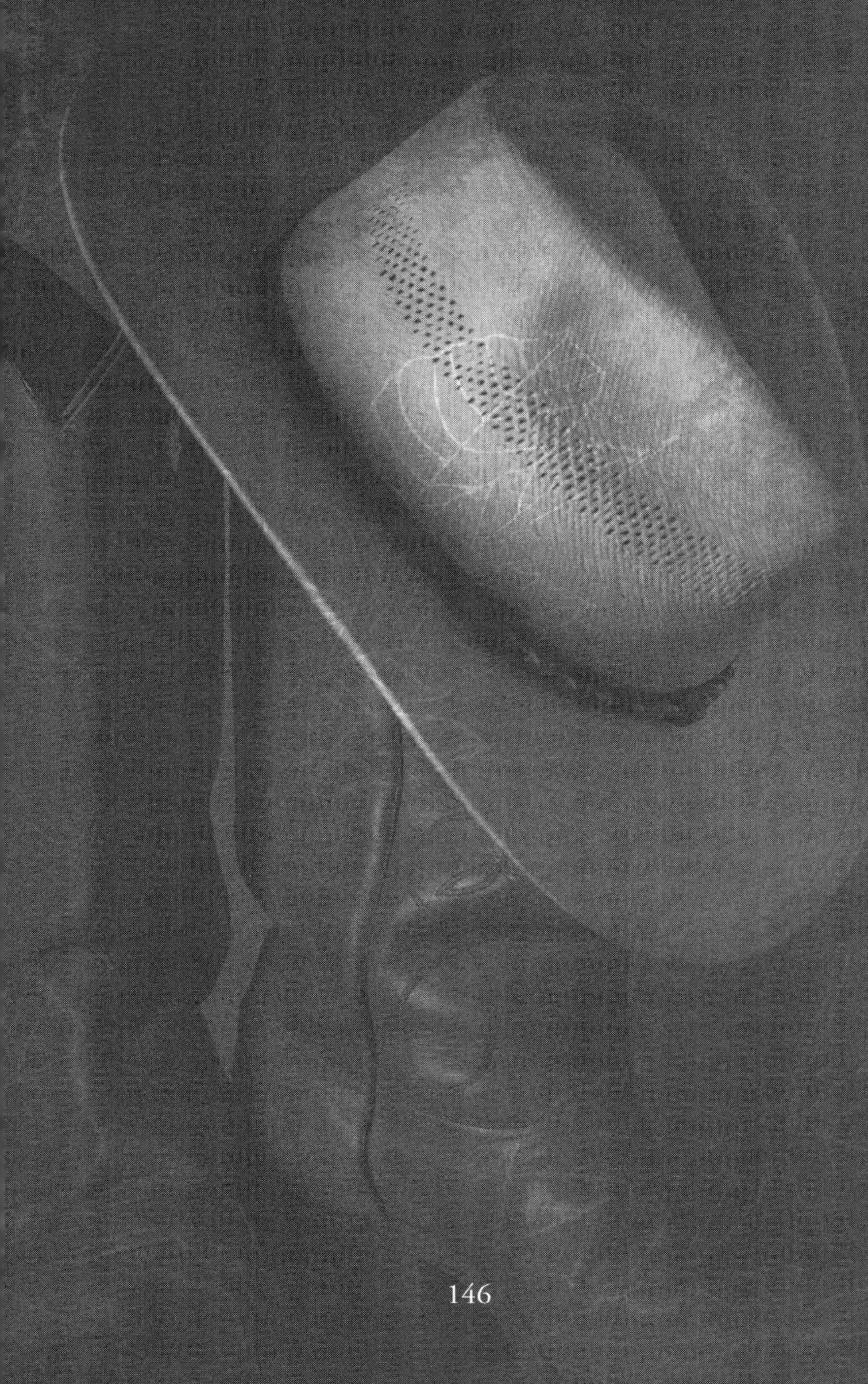

Chapter TWENTY

BLAISE

"You need to handle shit better, son," Garrett said over the line.

My gaze was on Madeline, curled up asleep on the bed. Not wanting to wake her, I moved to the stairs. She had fallen asleep in my arms after we got home.

"I saw the fucking feed from the cameras at the entrance. She was crying. That's my grandchild she's carrying. I told you about the pregnancy test because it's your job to keep her safe. If you can't do that, I'll have her moved into this house."

The moment Madeline had taken her purse and left the office today, Garrett had been alerted. He'd had her followed. Something I should have expected.

"The fuck you will," I growled. "She stays with me. I keep her safe. Her and my kid."

Garrett sighed. "Then, don't make her cry. That was fucking brutal to watch."

My hand gripped the phone tightly. I should have gotten away from the damn cameras before talking to her. I had been so tied up in knots about her keeping it a secret and not understanding why she would lie about it that I hadn't been thinking straight.

"She was emotional. I didn't make her cry," I replied, hating him for accusing me of it.

"You need to make a decision about Angel. She can't stay there, and you know it. This is going to upset her. Madeline doesn't need that." Garrett was only voicing what I'd already thought about.

"I know," I replied as I reached the top stair. "I'll talk to Gina tonight. I'm not sure she's going to want to move out with Angel."

"If she doesn't, I can hire a full-time nurse and sitter," he replied.

"It's time Gina has her freedom. She can't stay with Angel forever," I said.

"Agreed," Garrett sighed. Then, the line went silent.

I slipped the phone back into my pocket and went back down the stairs, not wanting to be away from her. Knowing she was carrying my baby made finding out what Liam was doing this close to her even more important. If he was a threat to her, I'd end him. I'd kill any son of a bitch that got too close to her.

Madeline was sitting up in bed with her arms wrapped around her knees when I walked back around the corner. Her hair hung over her shoulders. She looked so fucking young. Soon, she would be twenty, and I was already making her a mother.

"Hey," I said as I walked over to the bed.

Her face looked flushed when she lifted her eyes to meet mine.

"Did I wake you up?" I asked her.

"No," she said, then bit her bottom lip.

Why did she look embarrassed? What was I missing?

I sat down on the bed and reached over to tuck some hair behind her ear so I could see her face clearly.

She shivered, and goose bumps covered her bare arms.

"Are you cold?"

She shook her head.

I ran a finger down her arm. "These aren't from being cold?"

"No," she replied.

I moved my hand to her calf and pulled it toward me, opening her legs, then ran my hand up the inside of her thigh. She shivered again. My cock pressed against the zipper of my jeans. When my fingertips reached the crotch of her panties, I felt the dampness.

"No, this isn't cold at all," I told her before slipping a finger under the satin fabric.

She sucked in a sharp breath, and I watched as her eyes fluttered closed. My girl was horny. Her slick entrance felt swollen as the warmth of her arousal coated my fingers. It was different down here, I realized.

Why hadn't I figured this out sooner? When I'd buried my face between her thighs two nights ago and eaten her like a man possessed, why hadn't I noticed?

I stood then and grabbed the sides of her panties and pulled them down. She was in one of my shirts. When we had gotten home, I'd undressed her and slipped this over her before having her lie down and rest. Seeing her in my clothes made the possessive monster inside of me calm down. It eased me.

Tossing the panties to the floor, I pressed her back, opening her to me. I took in the view. She always had me so fucking out of control that I hadn't taken the time to realize her body was changing.

"What are you doing?" she asked. I could hear the uncertainty in her voice.

I lifted my gaze from her sweet, hot cunt to her beautiful eyes. "Looking at this pussy I own and how it's changing."

She blushed then and covered her face with her hands. "Don't do that," she pleaded.

I slid my hand up her thigh, then ran a finger through the swollen pink folds.

Madeline let out a gasp and jerked. "Ah!"

I smiled as I slid a finger inside and felt her muscles clench as it pulled at my finger. Even as her hips moved toward me, she kept her face covered.

"Look at me," I told her.

"No. It's embarrassing. Do I—does it … is it weird now?"

I reached up and pulled her hands from her face, forcing her to meet my gaze. "It's hot, swollen, pink, and smells like heaven," I said. "Now, lie back because I need to taste you."

She blinked several times, as if she was unsure.

"Now, Madeline," I demanded.

She inhaled, and her breasts bounced under my shirt as her hard nipples showed through the soft fabric. When she lay back, I moved in and slowly began to lick her from back to front. Her soft cries and moans made it taste even sweeter.

"Please," she begged as I continued my slow pace. "Blaise, please!"

I pressed a kiss to her clit, and she jumped, then cried out, "Oh God!"

"What does my girl want?" I asked her, then slid my tongue inside her entrance.

"I need you," she breathed.

"What do you need?" I asked her, continuing to enjoy her sweetness on my tongue.

"Fuck me," she moaned.

She was learning. I grinned as I gave her one last lick, then sat back on my knees and began to undress while she watched me with hooded eyes. She didn't close her legs and kept my view of her wide open. Her hips shifted restlessly, and she panted.

"Hurry," she begged. "I need you inside me."

Damn. I stood up and discarded my jeans and briefs, then went back to cover her body with mine. The tip of my engorged cock pressed against her tight entrance, and I teased us both, loving her soft, little whimpers. They made me crazy.

When she lifted her hips, I thrust into her, filling her up hard and fast. She wasn't just swollen along the lips of her pussy. The tight little hole that brought me so much pleasure was even tighter.

"FUCK!" I growled as I began to pump inside her.

Her hands grabbed my arms, and she threw her head back as she cried out with each thrust of my hips. I had never seen anything sexier in my life. I could stay inside her, fucking this tight little snatch, for the rest of my life. Nothing else mattered.

"Oh! Oh! GOD!" she cried and began to tremble as her orgasm started breaking free.

"That's it, baby. Come for me," I said as she bucked beneath me and her nails bit into my arms.

I wasn't done. I wanted to feel her pleasure squeeze my dick one more time before I filled her.

I moved slower until her eyes opened and she blinked up at me, sated.

"Roll over and get on your hands and knees," I told her as I pulled out and moved back so she could do as she had been told.

She didn't ask questions and did exactly that. Her round ass was stuck up, and my hand itched to spank it. I did, and she cried out, then looked over her shoulder at me. I held her gaze as I slapped the other asscheek, then moved my eyes to see the pink handprint forming.

As much as I wanted to see her ass bright red from my hand, my dick was throbbing to sink back inside of her. My hands grabbed her hips, and I plunged back inside her, groaning loudly as she sucked me in tightly.

"Holy fuck, you feel good," I groaned. "Pussy shouldn't be this damn addictive."

She cried out as I began to slam into her harder. I wanted her to feel me the next day. To know that her pussy was sore because I'd fucked it thoroughly. She cried out my name, and the sound of it made me want to beat on my chest.

"What are you doing to me, woman?" I growled out.

"I'm gonna come again," she shouted as the wave hit her and she began to tremble underneath me.

The spasm in her inner walls pulled my release from me. I pumped my hips as my sperm shot out, filling her over and over.

"GAAAAHHHH!" I roared as the intensity shook me.

Every nerve in my body tingled as I came down from the euphoria only Madeline could give me.

I pulled out of her slowly, and when she started to fall onto the bed, I grabbed her ass and held it up, opening her legs with my knee.

"I want to see my cum leaking out of you," I told her.

"Oh," she said breathlessly. "Why?"

I ran a finger over her slit. "Because you've made me fucking crazy. I feel like a Neanderthal. I want to mark you and see my seed in your cunt."

She shivered at my touch, and I let her go so she could fall onto the bed. The possessive monster she brought out in me needed to let her rest. I could fuck her again later. I would fuck her again later.

Lying down beside her, I pulled her back against my chest and kept my arm wrapped around her waist. "Even if I wasn't so fucking in love with you, I'd be owned by your pussy," I admitted to her.

Her body shook as she laughed softly.

Smiling, I closed my eyes and let myself be content. It was a rare thing.

Chapter TWENTY-ONE

MADELINE

Blaise had held my hair back as I threw up this morning. Then, he wiped my face clean with a cool cloth before carrying me back to bed and bringing me a glass of ice water. He was so gentle with me that it made me tear up, but I was finding that I did that a lot these days. Crying and nausea were becoming common for me.

When he pressed a kiss to my forehead and told me to rest until he got home, I sat up and said I needed to go to work. However, Garrett wasn't allowing that the rest of the week. Blaise said that until the vomiting stopped in the mornings, Garrett didn't want me coming into work until it eased. Even if that was lunchtime.

While I had been aware how ridiculous they were being, I'd been too tired to argue.

The next time I opened my eyes, I reached for my phone, but it wasn't there. I sat up and yawned, then looked around to see where I had left it. Reaching for the television remote,

I turned on the massive flat screen to see what time it was that way—11:23 a.m.

Well, crap. I'd slept for four more hours.

Hoping Blaise was upstairs, I hurried to get a shower and get dressed. Other than being hungry, I was fine. Maybe that meant I could go to the office today. I had just started back, and I didn't want to get behind on things.

When I reached the top step, I realized I never found my phone and glanced back down the stairs but decided it was possible Blaise had it. Besides, I wasn't leaving right now. Unlocking the door, I stepped into the main part of the house and closed the door behind me. There were no voices coming from the kitchen, but then breakfast had been over with for hours. The guys had all gone to their jobs.

Stepping into the kitchen, I found Gina sitting at the table, texting on her phone with a bottle of water in front of her. She smiled brightly at me. "Hey, sleepyhead," she said. "I was about to text Blaise to see if he had a key hidden so I could go make sure you were alive down there."

I laughed. "Sorry. I didn't mean to sleep that late."

She shrugged. "Wish I could sleep like that. I have terrible insomnia," she told me. "Anyway, Blaise left your phone on the counter. He had to do some update to it or something. He also sent you a text, according to what he just told me."

I looked at the phone, relieved I hadn't lost it. "Thanks. I couldn't figure out where it went."

I picked it up and opened it to read his text.

GOOD MORNING, BABY. I HOPE YOU SLEPT WELL. I'VE PUT A NEW TRACKING SYSTEM IN YOUR PHONE, SO PLEASE KEEP IT ON YOU. GINA IS GOING TO TAKE YOU TO GET LUNCH AND DO SOME SHOPPING. I'LL HAVE SOMEONE SHADOWING THE TWO OF YOU TO KEEP YOU PROTECTED, BUT YOU WON'T SEE THEM

OR FEEL SMOTHERED. GO HAVE FUN. YOU NEED A BREAK.

I smiled down at the text. He was trying to give me some freedom. He did listen to me. Even when he was angry about it and scowling. I lifted my gaze from the phone to see Gina grinning at me.

"I'm ready when you are," I told her, although I didn't plan on buying anything.

I was not going to spend Blaise's money, and he had bought me more clothes than any one woman needed. I would enjoy watching Gina shop though. Going out with a female friend and having lunch wasn't something I was accustomed to. I'd been out with Melanie, but that was different. This felt like I had a friend.

Gina sent a text and then stood up. "I need to get out! I am so glad he agreed to this," she admitted. "Life here all the time with Angel can be tiring." Her voice sounded sad just then.

I wondered if she ever got a life outside of being with Angel or taking care of the guys. It didn't seem fair, and it also sounded lonely. This would be good for both of us.

We didn't take my SUV, which surprised me. I knew it had a tracker, but I assumed so did Gina's car. It was a black sedan with tinted windows. I imagined it stood out less. I'd sent Blaise a text, thanking him for today, but he hadn't responded yet. It always made me nervous when he was silent. Believing he was invincible was hard. Everyone else acted as if he couldn't be hurt, but he was human, and he was always a target.

My stomach growled, and I winced.

Gina laughed. "We'll eat first," she said, glancing over at me before she turned left at a red light that I was used to turning right at.

Today, I would see more of the city. What I had seen was limited.

Gina turned on some music. It was some alternative stuff I wasn't familiar with, and she began to tap the steering wheel like they were drums. I turned to look out the window, seeing more open land than anything. It didn't feel like we were driving into town. If anything, it felt like we were driving away from it.

I started to ask Gina and saw her glance in the rearview mirror. I turned to look behind us, and a black SUV was following us. Must be our shadow we weren't supposed to see. I glanced back at Gina, who was smiling. She must be thinking the same thing.

If the guy who was keeping us safe didn't see anything wrong with where we were headed, then I was overthinking it. Blaise had made me paranoid. Besides, it was Gina. She was part of the family. I was fine.

Just as I had that thought, Gina slowed and turned onto a dirt road. The hair on the back of my neck stood up. Something was wrong. I could feel the change in the vehicle. Gina opened her door and gave me a smile that wasn't friendly at all. It looked more like she'd won something from me.

"Get out," she said.

I didn't move, but watched as the black SUV pulled up beside her. She walked over to it, and the window rolled down on the passenger side. I could see her talking to whoever it was. My attention was so focused in on her mouth and trying to figure out what she was saying that when my door was jerked open, I didn't even have time to scream before I was gagged and pulled from the car. My eyes went to the purse sitting on the floorboard. My phone was in there. I panicked, kicking my legs, trying to get free.

"You're fine. Easy, sweet thing," the deep male voice said in my ear. "I don't want to hurt you."

He didn't? Then, what did he want to do with me? Rape me? Oh God, no. I was pregnant. The baby. What would they do when they found out I was pregnant?

I began to struggle against him again, but he was stronger than I was, and it did little good.

Gina opened up the back door of the SUV for him, and he put me inside, took a rope, then began to tie my wrists together before taking the rope and tying it to the seat in front of me. I tried to wiggle my hands, but there was no budging.

"Don't pull on them. It'll make them tighter, and I don't want those pretty little wrists raw," he said, making my stomach twist in a sick knot.

Then, he proceeded to buckle me up. It surprised me so much that I froze and watched him. What was going on? He had me gagged, my hands tied, and he was worried about my safety?

"She can't ever come back. If he knows I handed her over, he'll kill me," Gina said to the driver.

I stared at her in horror. What had she done?

"He won't get her back," the man replied, then rolled up the window.

I watched as Gina got inside her car and started to drive away. When my purse was tossed from her window into the grass, I cried out behind my gag. That was my only way to get to Blaise. There was no other way he could find me.

"It's fine, sugar. No one is going to hurt you," the driver said.

I jerked my gaze from my purse, now left in the tall grass where Gina's car had been parked, to the man. He was big. As in tall and broad shoulders. His hair was in a ponytail and almost black. Tattoos covered his bare arms, and I would guess the rest of him, where the leather vest covered him, was too. I saw several rings on his fingers, and the dark sunglasses he wore covered his eyes.

I was the furthest thing from fine. I had been abducted, and someone I had trusted had handed me over. Blaise wouldn't know what had happened to me. He'd track my phone and find my purse in the grass. That was it. Nothing else.

"You should be careful who you trust," the guy in the passenger seat said.

No shit. I was very aware of that at the moment.

"Don't worry. You're safe now. No traitorous bitches where we are going," he added.

Where was that? I wanted to know.

"Probably need to blindfold her," the driver told him. "Until she accepts things, she could tell someone where she is."

Accepts what? I didn't want to be blindfolded. I shook my head, silently pleading with them not to do that.

The guy in the passenger seat looked back at me, and his pale green eyes almost seemed friendly. Maybe they would be if he wasn't a kidnapper with tattoos also covering his body and dreadlocks in his brown hair.

"She looks fucking terrified," he said, looking truly sorry for that. Then, he flicked his tongue across his top teeth as he decided what to do with me, and the silver in his tongue caught the light. His tongue was pierced.

"She can't see, Tex. You know that," the driver muttered.

Pierced tongue with the green eyes was named Tex. I needed to remember this. At some point, I would find a way to contact Blaise. When I did, I needed all the information I could give him.

"Fuck," Tex muttered, then winked at me. "I swear you'll be safe. Just making sure we don't let you see something that could cause more trouble than any of us want."

I screamed behind the gag that they had already done that. Blaise was going to be furious. Did they not know who he was? They had to know. This had to be to get to him. But why?

"Easy there, sugar. You'll make yourself hoarse. No need for all that," the driver told me.

I glared at him. I wasn't his sugar.

He chuckled. "She's a little fireball."

A phone rang then, and the driver pressed the screen. I couldn't see what it said from where I was sitting.

"We got her," the driver said.

"Is she hurt?" a deep voice asked, sounding as if he actually cared.

"No," the driver replied. "Angry as hell, but she's not hurt."

There was a low chuckle on the other line. "I'd expect that."

"Brick wants to blindfold her, but she looks terrified. I can't bring myself to do it," Tex said, glancing back at me.

Brick was the driver's name. I needed to study his face closer with his glasses off so I could describe him in more detail when I got the chance.

"Not yet. No need. You're going south with her. Can she hear me?" the man on the line asked.

"Yeah," Brick replied. "She's listening."

"Madeline, you're okay. No one is going to hurt you. I'd kill anyone who tried. These are two of my best men. They will get you here safely."

I didn't want to go to him at all. I wanted to go home. I wanted Blaise. I tried to yell that through the gag.

"Did you fucking gag her?" the man asked.

"Brick told me to," Tex said quickly.

"She was going to scream when we moved her from the car the bitch had her in to our Ranger," Brick said.

"Jesus, Brick. You could have ungagged her once she was in the vehicle with you."

Tex looked back at me and raised his eyebrows, then grinned. If I wasn't being abducted by these men, I might think he was funny. But seeing as he was my kidnapper, I hated him. I watched as he unbuckled, and the SUV came to a stop. Tex climbed out of the vehicle, then opened my door and loosened the gag around me before taking it off. We were on a long, deserted stretch of road. I could yell for help, but it would be a waste of my voice. I needed to save it for when it would count.

"She's ungagged," Tex announced as he got back in the front seat and closed the door.

Brick pulled back onto the road and started driving.

"Madeline," the voice over the phone said.

"Yes," I replied tightly.

I needed to get all the information I could. I would get free. I would get back to Blaise. I had to for me and the baby inside me.

"My name is Liam Walsh," he said.

Everything inside me stilled. I didn't even take a breath. I had never heard his last name, but I had heard his first.

"Do you know who I am?" he asked.

I gasped as I inhaled oxygen again. "Yes," I choked out.

"Then, they know who I am," he said with a heavy sigh.

It was silent for a moment. I waited for the man whose DNA I shared to speak again.

"I'm sorry, honey. They're going to have to blindfold you after all. If they know who I am, then they'll know where to look first," Liam said to me.

"The bitch didn't tell you that, I assume, Tex," His tone changed when he addressed Tex.

"No, she didn't," he replied.

"Where are you taking me?" I asked him.

"I've looked for you for almost twenty years. It's time I got to know my daughter. It's time you came home," Liam replied.

"You aren't my home," I all but shouted.

He had taken me from my home. He had taken me from Blaise.

"Fair enough. But I am your father, and I don't know what lies you've been told, but I loved Etta. Your mother was the only woman I've ever loved. You're all I have left of her. I want to get to know you," he told me.

There was a sadness in his voice that made his words seem sincere.

A battle waged inside me. I had a real father. One who was telling me a much different story than the one I had heard from Garrett. The little girl inside of me who wanted a father who loved her fought against the woman who already had a man she belonged to.

Chapter TWENTY-TWO

MADELINE

I woke up, blinking against the blindfold that I still wore. Keeping still, I didn't want to alert them that I was awake.

The radio was playing "Livin' on a Prayer" by Bon Jovi. Neither Tex nor Brick was talking. The slowing, then speeding up of the vehicle told me we were in a city. No longer on back roads.

A phone started to ring, but it ended quickly.

"Yeah," I heard Tex whisper. "About an hour out."

He let out a low chuckle. "She's fucking gorgeous."

"Ouch," he said sharply. "What the fuck, Brick?"

"Don't talk about her like that," Brick said in a low voice.

"It's just Country. He asked me what she looked like. Jesus," Tex said.

What kind of names were these? Tex, Brick, Country?

"She's asleep. Yeah," Tex said softly.

"Mmhmm," he said, not giving me any information at all.

"See you there."

"Liam hears you call her fucking gorgeous, and he'll feed you your balls," Brick warned him.

"Shit, might be worth it," he replied.

"Careful," Brick said, sounding angry.

"It ain't me you need to be warning. Just wait until Micah sees her," Tex whispered.

"He's not that insane," Brick replied.

"You sure about that?" Tex asked.

They fell silent after that and gave me time to think.

Blaise didn't know that Liam had found me. He'd have told me if he knew. He didn't even know where to find Liam. The only way I was going to see him again was if I could convince Liam that I had to go back. Maybe telling him about the fact that I was pregnant would help. If this wasn't a lie and Liam wanted to get to know me, then I could talk to Blaise. Explain things to him. Perhaps the family and whatever organization Liam was in could make a truce.

Who was I kidding? Liam had taken me. Blaise was going to kill everyone. They needed to know that. My father, or whatever I was supposed to call him, had signed his death certificate. I wasn't sure even I could save him.

"Does Liam know who Blaise is?" I asked them as I sat up straight in my seat. My hands were still tied up and connected to the seat in front of me. I was careful not to tug on them though. They didn't hurt, and I didn't want to make them start hurting.

"Yep," Brick replied.

"Then, he knows Blaise will kill all of you," I said matter-of-factly.

"Possibly," Brick replied. "But highly unlikely. He would have to come on our turf, and that evens the playing field."

I sighed, wondering if Blaise would know where this turf was.

"How long have we been on the road?" I asked.

"Not telling you that. The less you know, the better," he told me.

"Your wrists okay?" Tex asked me then. "We'll be there soon, and you won't have to deal with them any longer."

"They're fine," I muttered.

What was Blaise doing now? He had to have figured out I was gone. Had he found my phone and purse on the side of that road? He would be terrified. My eyes watered as I thought about how he was feeling. I knew I wasn't going to die or be raped. There was that at least. He, however, had no idea if I was even alive. My chest ached for him until it hurt to breathe.

"Liam's looked for you for as long as I've known him. He's a good man," Tex said in a reassuring voice.

Knowing my real father had wanted to find me would be more comforting if he wasn't in some drug cartel or whatever.

"I'm sure all cartel members are good men," I replied sarcastically.

Tex let out a laugh. "Cartel? Who the fuck told you that? Liam isn't in the fucking cartel. We don't touch drugs. Not our shit." He sounded honestly amused.

"So, you're telling me, you aren't part of organized crime?" I asked, although I had to admit, the tattoos, piercings, leather vests didn't look like the wealth I'd seen within the family.

"That's the fucking Mafia. Not us," Tex said. "I'm sure they'd like you to think that we are part of that world though."

I stayed silent. He didn't sound like he was lying, but then what did I know? I had trusted Gina. Apparently, I had no idea when I was being lied to.

"What is it that you do then? Since you aren't scared that you just took the future boss's woman away from a powerful Mafia family?" I asked.

"Clubs. We have clubs," Brick answered instead.

"What kind of clubs?" I asked him, knowing he wanted Tex to stop telling me things.

"The kind that make money," he clipped. "That's all you are getting from us. You can ask Liam whatever you want."

I sighed and bent my head to rub my chin on my arm. It itched, and I was still without use of my hands.

"How much longer?" I asked then.

"Almost there," Tex replied.

I remained silent until the vehicle came to a stop and I heard the guys opening their doors. When my door opened, I expected the blindfold to come off, but my hands were the first to be freed. I sighed in relief.

"Sorry about that," Tex said.

I felt his hand rub my free wrists to soothe them. I jerked my hands away from him, not wanting his touch. He chuckled, then unbuckled me. I reached up to take the blindfold off, but his hand grabbed mine.

"Not yet."

"Why?" I snapped at him.

"We need to get inside first, sugar," Brick said from somewhere nearby.

Of course I couldn't see the building we were going into. That might help me when I found a way to get in touch with Blaise. However, I had every intention of convincing Liam to let me talk to Blaise. I at least needed him to know I was alive and okay.

I stumbled in the heeled sandals I was wearing, and hands grabbed my waist to steady me.

"Easy," Tex said near my ear.

"If I had known Gina was taking me to my abduction instead of lunch and shopping, I would have dressed more appropriately," I replied.

I heard another male chuckle from a distance.

"God, you sound like Etta," Liam said.

I paused then. I wasn't sure how I felt about this. He had loved my mother. Or he had claimed to love her. Why did I want to believe he had so badly? I was a girl with daddy issues. That was clear.

"Let's go. Almost inside," Tex said to me.

I continued on, and a hand closed over mine and pulled me inside an air-conditioned building. Then, the blindfold was taken away, and my eyes met a pair of hazel eyes. He smiled, and something about that smile was familiar. As if I had seen it before, but I hadn't since I'd never seen the man in my life.

He looked similar to Brick and Tex. Long hair pulled back in a ponytail, tattoos, leather vest.

"Jesus, you look just like her," he said as he looked at me.

"I've heard that," I replied, not wanting to care that this was my real father.

He grinned. "You've got her spunk."

I felt guilty. I felt like I was betraying Blaise by suddenly wanting to be here. I wanted to ask this man questions about my mother. About him. About their time together. Things that I'd never thought I'd get a chance to know. I missed Blaise, and I wanted to go back to him. But I wanted to know about my parents. Their history.

My stomach growled loudly. I hadn't eaten all day. I didn't know what time it was now, but I was hungry.

Liam's brows snapped together. "Did you fucking starve my daughter?" he barked.

"She fell asleep," Brick replied.

"Have Goldie fix her something. Not taking her in the kitchen or near the others tonight. She's had enough for today," Liam said to someone behind me. He shifted his gaze back to me. "Come with me," he said. "I'll show you your room."

My room?

I looked around. This was not a house. It didn't look like one anyway. The walls were black as we walked down a hallway and then up a flight of stairs. Once we came to the top, things weren't as dark, but they weren't bright and welcoming either. There was a wide, long hallway going left to right. I counted four doors on each side. The walls were a navy blue, and the floor was a dark, almost-black wood. The lighting was on the walls instead of the ceiling. It reminded me of a castle in a storybook, but instead of lanterns, there were actual sconces on the walls.

"This way," Liam told me, and we turned left at the top of the stairs.

Two doors down, he stopped and opened the door. Inside was a large room with a queen-size bed with a tall white wooden headboard. The quilt on the bed was white with flowers on it in different patterns. The walls were lilac instead of the dark colors I'd seen everywhere else. There was a dresser with a television hanging on the wall above it and a door that I assumed led to a closet. On the other side of the room was an open door that led into a bathroom.

"This is yours. You can change it any way you'd like. I want you to be comfortable here," Liam told me.

I wouldn't be staying, but I didn't say that. I had a lot to figure out. I wanted to go back to Blaise, but I wanted to find out about my beginning. What my parents had been like, what had happened, his side of the story.

"This is nice," I replied.

He smiled. "Come this way. Let's get you fed and talk some."

I followed him back into the hallway, and this time, we turned right and went all the way to the end. I hadn't noticed the door at the end. It blended in with the walls. Liam opened it, and we walked into what looked like a large living room or perhaps a gathering room. There was a pool table, a bar, two black leather sofas, and a television. Some bookshelves on the far-right wall were full, and I wondered what men covered in tattoos read.

"This is what we call the library," he said and waved his hand toward the sofas. "Please, have a seat."

Chapter TWENTY-THREE

BLAISE

"Where the fuck is he then?" I roared as I picked up a lamp to my right and threw it against the wall.

"Liam left yesterday," Huck said. "Gage is headed to Miami to check the clubs that The Judgment owns. He'll find someone who knows where Liam is."

I slammed my fist into the wall. The rage inside of me was consuming me. I would kill every person involved. Every motherfucker who touched her. She was mine, and somehow, they'd taken her right from under my nose. Which meant there was a traitor among us. The same fucker who had put that envelope at her door. I was going to kill them. Slowly. They would suffer, and I would laugh while I watched it.

"Angel is screaming," Gina said behind me. "You're scaring her."

"Then, take her to Garrett's!" I yelled at her. I needed Gina out of my sight anyway. "Go with her. Stay there. I don't want to look at you."

I heard her sharp intake of breath. When she didn't move, the fury inside me felt like it was going to burst out of my chest.

"GO! I can't fucking look at you!"

She turned and ran from the room then.

The cameras in the house hadn't shown anything unusual. I could see where Madeline had gotten ready, but then nothing. It was as if Madeline had never been here, like she had disappeared. When I had tracked her phone, I had found it downstairs, under the fucking sofa. She wouldn't have put it there. I had texted her good morning and told her I loved her. She responded immediately saying she loved me too. Then things had gotten busy and I hadn't texted anything more. Those were the only text she had received and sent today.

Gina had sworn she saw nothing. Heard nothing. The cameras had shown Gina leaving through the gate in her car with those fucking black tinted windows. She never used the car, and she knew there was no tracker on it.

She was lying to me, and I swore to God if she had anything to do with this, I would shoot her between the eyes and walk away.

"You don't know Gina did anything," Levi said.

"No, I don't. But it's a fucking coincidence that the cameras were manipulated again, and we don't even see proof Madeline was in this house on the video feed. If Gina didn't do this, then she'll get to live. But I'm gonna need some solid proof this time," I replied.

"If Liam took her, then she's safe. She's his daughter. He won't kill her or rape her."

Levi was trying to calm me down. Nothing would calm me down.

"He took my woman," I said, glaring at him. "And she's pregnant with my baby."

"Fuuuck," Levi replied, his eyes going wide.

I hadn't told any of them that yet. I was still digesting it myself.

"Jesus Christ," Huck swore.

I stalked toward the door. "I want her found. I want her back here in my bed. Gina and Angel need to be moved out. Even if Gina had nothing to do with this, I can't look at her. I don't want her around me. She was the only person who could tell me something, and she swears she knows nothing. I won't ever fucking believe that. There was no one else in this house."

I stopped when I reached the door and gripped the handle so tightly that I felt as if I could crush it in my hand. "If it isn't Liam," I said as my chest felt like a boulder had slammed into it, "if she is hurt or—" I stopped. I couldn't even say the word. Not about Madeline. I was supposed to protect her, and she'd been taken from me. "No one is safe because nothing will matter to me anymore."

I jerked open the door and headed for my truck. I had to get to Miami. I wasn't fucking waiting on Gage to report back. Standing here while time ticked by was going to make me go insane.

I heard the door open behind me. I looked back to see Huck coming toward me.

"Levi can deal with things here. I'm going with you," he said.

I didn't argue. If I found Liam, I would need backup because I wasn't waiting on Garrett to send an army.

Chapter TWENTY-FOUR

MADELINE

The lasagna, salad, and garlic bread were enough for two people, but I managed to eat it all. Liam drank a glass of whiskey while he watched me. He didn't ask questions while I ate, and I was thankful for that. I was ravenous.

When I put the fork down and met his gaze, he looked concerned. "Was Blaise starving you?"

"No. I was kidnapped before I got a chance to eat anything today," I replied sourly.

It was his fault I had not eaten.

He winced. "Damn. I should have made sure they fed you."

"It would have been hard to eat with my hands tied and a blindfold on," I countered.

He shrugged. "True."

The door opened then, and in walked someone new. He was tall, had less tattoos than the others, was wearing a snug navy T-shirt, a pair of jeans, and brown boots. His dirty-blond hair almost looked ginger and was tucked behind his ears. The face on him was that of a magazine or billboard advertisement. Thick black eyelashes, pale blue eyes, a strong jawline, ripped muscles.

He was studying me as well, and the hint of a smile that played across his lips made me feel uncomfortable. I wasn't flirting, nor was I attracted to him. He was a beautiful male, but I was in love with a superior beautiful male.

"Micah, that's my daughter." Liam's tone was a warning.

Micah seemed unaffected. "I know," he drawled, not taking his eyes off me.

"Madeline, this is Micah. Keep your distance. He's a whore," my father informed me.

I raised my eyebrows at that description. "I see," I replied.

Micah's grin turned up. "I heard she was a fireball, but they left out that she was a complete fucking smokeshow too."

"That's because they all know that my daughter is off-limits, and you think with your dick," Liam told him. "Go expend some of that energy at River Styx tonight. I need someone there. I'm keeping Brick here to watch things for me."

Micah bit his lip as he continued to look at me. I glared back at him with disgust.

"Our girls are hot, but they don't look like her," he said.

"MICAH!" Liam raised his voice. "You can leave now."

He had the audacity to wink at me before he turned and left the room. Once he was gone, Liam looked back to me.

"I'm sorry about him. His father was my closest friend. We grew up together. He started The Judgment with me. When he died, Micah was twelve. He's not had a mother to help, and he's been raised inside the club. He is now my VP, like his father was. Stay clear of him though."

There was no need for him to worry. I wasn't available to be interested. My heart and soul were already claimed.

"What is The Judgment? I'm guessing an organization or a club, but what kind?" I asked him.

"MC," he replied.

I continued to stare at him. I wasn't sure what an MC was.

"Motorcycle club," he clarified when it was obvious I was confused.

"So, those are real," I said.

He chuckled. "As real as the Mafia."

Point taken.

"He's going to come get me, and he'll kill anyone in his way," I told Liam.

Liam nodded. "I'm aware of who Blaise Hughes is. I don't want my daughter in that life. It's dangerous. You're a target. The Hughes have many enemies, Madeline."

As if I hadn't already known all this.

"I love him. You can't decide who I'm with. I'm an adult now," I pointed out.

"I just found you. I'm not going to let your life be shortened because someone has a vendetta with Blaise. You're young. I can give you a life that's free of danger. You can truly live without having to be protected constantly."

My temples pounded, and I was grinding my teeth. I wanted to hear about my mom and how she had ended up pregnant and on the run. I didn't want to be told that he thought he could give me a better life. One I was not in need of, nor did I want it.

"I don't want another life," I replied. "Blaise is it for me." I stood up then, not allowing him to argue with me.

He didn't know me, and I hadn't come to him willingly. I hadn't been searching for a dad.

"It's been a long day, and I'm tired."

He stood up. "Of course. We can talk tomorrow."

I walked to the door and stopped before opening it. "I need to talk to him before he shows up and kills everyone. He needs to know I'm alive and safe."

Liam rubbed his beard with one hand. "If I can get you an untraceable phone so you can speak to him, will that ease your mind?"

I nodded. "Do it soon. Before people die," I replied, then opened the door.

"What makes you think he's willing to kill for you?" Liam asked me.

I turned back to him. "Because he's done it before. He had the men who I thought were my father and brother killed when he found out that they were going to sell me to a sex trafficker to pay their debts. I was abducted by one of his enemies from a movie theater, and the two men who had taken me were killed and hung on a cross."

Liam looked surprised. "I want to know about this man you thought was your father," he said with an edge to his voice.

"I'll tell you about Luke tomorrow," I replied. "But I want to know about my mom."

"Of course," he replied.

Chapter TWENTY-FIVE

MADELINE

I wasn't even at the door of my room when Tex came running up the stairs.

"LIAM!" he called out.

Liam had been walking me to my room. He turned back to look at Tex.

Tex put his hands on his knees as he gasped for breath. Where had he run from? One flight of stairs couldn't have been that difficult. Tex looked back at me, then turned back to Liam.

"Toxic Throttle," he said. "Grinder called. They've had visitors. No one was killed, but the threat was made clear. Butch said the wrong thing, and he had a knife at his throat, and the crazy motherfucker sliced it enough to break blood. Grinder went for the gun, and before he could get it out, he was shot in the arm. He said he was going to start killing if Maddy wasn't handed over, and then he left."

That sounded like Gage. Out of the three men in the family that solely worked for Blaise, Gage was the craziest. My eyes shot to Liam.

He nodded his head. “Let the others know to get extra security in place. Get me an untraceable now. She needs to call him.”

Tex nodded and turned to run down the stairs.

“He called you Maddy,” he asked.

“It’s not Blaise. It’s one of his men. Blaise wouldn’t have left anyone alive,” I told him. “And he never calls me Maddy.” I opened the door and stepped into the room.

My heart was hammering in my chest. I had expected this, but knowing that my father might get killed made me nervous. I paced the room, waiting on the phone to arrive. Calming Blaise down was important. I wanted to go home to him, too, but I also wanted to learn about my father. My mother. There were too many questions I hadn’t asked yet. Getting Blaise to see that I needed this would be hard after the way I had been taken right out from under his protection.

I chewed on my bottom lip, worried that this was going to be harder than a simple phone call. Garrett wouldn’t be happy either. This made the family look weak. I understood that, and I wasn’t sure anything I said would stop Garrett even if it could slow down Blaise. Also, there was Gina. Blaise was going to want to know how they had taken me, and if I told him about Gina … I wasn’t sure she’d get to live. Handing me over to them had been wrong, but she didn’t deserve to die. She’d given me to my biological father, not a sex trafficker. Gina had wanted me gone. I wasn’t sure why, but she had. Part of that had to be my fault.

The door to the room opened, and Liam walked in with Tex and Brick behind him.

He held out a small phone to me. “Call him,” he said.

“Get the fucker to stop shooting folks. Jesus,” Tex said angrily.

I glared at him. “They lived, didn’t they?”

"Still fucking overkill," Tex replied.

"If it had been Blaise, they'd be dead," I told him, then dialed Blaise's number into the phone.

"This had better be Walsh." Blaise's voice was deadly.

"It's me," I said, feeling my stomach twist.

I hated hearing him like this. They heard a monster. I heard the man I loved terrified.

"Madeline." He breathed out my name in relief. "Where are you? Whose fucking phone is this? I also want to know how the bastard got you. I'm gonna kill whoever handed you over."

I swallowed. He couldn't kill Gina. It would be hard for him. She was like his sister. I would ignore that for now.

"I'm with Liam, it's a burner phone I believe, and I can't tell you that," I hoped he didn't push me.

"Are you hurt?" he barked out.

"I am fine. No one has hurt me. I wasn't hurt when I was taken. But I need you to call off the guys. They're"—I looked over at Liam and the others, and I wouldn't give them any of the family's names—"hurting people. There is no need for that. Those are innocent people who don't know where I am."

Blaise let out a string of curses. "I don't care. Until I have you in my fucking arms, they can all die. Where are you, Madeline?"

I looked around the room. "I honestly don't know. But please, Blaise, let me explain. Just stop them from hurting anyone else until I explain."

Blaise made a low growl, and I knew he didn't like what I was asking.

"Tell Gage to stop. Wait. I'm talking to her now. No more moves until I'm done," he ordered to someone with him.

"Talk to me, baby. I'm losing my goddamn mind," he said into the phone.

"Like I said, I am fine. I'm being treated well. I would have called sooner, but Liam didn't realize the importance until …" I paused, remembering not to say Gage's name. "Uh, well, one of his people was shot and another apparently got a little cut to the throat."

"Good girl," he said, realizing I was protecting Gage's identity.

Why his praise made me feel as if I had won something, I didn't know. We were discussing Gage, who would kill in cold blood and walk away, smoking a cigarette.

"Liam does have you then." Blaise wanted confirmation.

"Yes, he does. He is under the assumption that my being with you is dangerous, and he wants to protect me. I've explained that I love you and I'm aware of the dangers, but I want to know about my mother and him. I want to know about my history, Blaise."

"Don't ask me to let you stay there." His voice was strained. "Don't do this to me, Madeline."

"Not forever. No! I want to come home. I want you. I just need this. A few days to get to know him, find out about my mother and how they met. Things Garrett doesn't have the details of. Things Eli didn't know. This is the only way I can ever know. Also, I want to get to know him. He's …" I lifted my eyes from the phone to see Liam watching me. There was emotion there, one that someone wouldn't expect when looking at him. He was rough around the edges, where Blaise was smooth. Both could be deadly, but they lived in different worlds. "He's my father."

"Fuck," Blaise groaned.

He didn't want me to stay here. I knew that, and I hated asking him.

"Baby, I can't trust him. I don't know if he's safe yet."

"He is," I replied.

"Tell me, Madeline, the person who handed you over to him. Who took you from my motherfucking house and gave you to him? Did you trust that person?"

His question reminded me how naive I had already figured out I was.

"Yes," I whispered.

"Exactly," he replied. "You trust too easily. Now, tell me who took you from me."

I sighed. "I can't let you kill them. It would hurt you to do it."

"Madeline," he growled, "if I can't kill that motherfucker who has you right now, I need to kill someone. I'm on edge, baby. They've taken what is mine. You are mine, and you don't even know where the fuck you are. I can't get you. Tell me who betrayed me."

I closed my eyes tightly. I couldn't let him kill her. "I think they had reasons. Some that are worth listening to and understanding. I think maybe I played a role in it, and you need to give this person a chance. Not just kill because of betrayal."

"Taking you—taking the one fucking person I love—is a death sentence. They knew it when they took you." His tone sounded like the Mafia boss he would be one day.

"Blaise, give me a few days. Then, I will have Liam bring me back to you," I told him. "If I'm not returned in three days"—I lifted my gaze to Liam's—"then unleash them. Let them kill until they find me."

Liam's eyes widened at my words, but I knew he needed to understand that I did not intend to let him keep me here. I belonged with Blaise. I also needed to find a way to save Gina's life.

"Give the son of a bitch the phone," Blaise bit out.

I held the phone toward Liam. "He wants to speak to you."

Liam took the phone from me and held it to his ear.

"Hughes," he said.

I watched his expression and saw it tense as his eyes narrowed. I wished Blaise had at least attempted to be nice or slightly cordial. There was my naivety again, rearing its head.

"She's my daughter."

I saw a slight drop to his shoulders, as if something Blaise had said made sense.

"I see. I was unaware of that. Thank you," he said, and this time, it was my eyes that widened.

"I didn't think you did," Liam replied, a smirk on his lips.

I wished I could hear what Blaise was saying.

Liam's gaze shot to me then. "No, she hasn't. I wouldn't let anything happen to her." He looked concerned. "Agreed."

Liam held the phone back out to me.

I took it and quickly put it back to my ear. "I'm here."

He inhaled sharply, and I knew he was struggling with whatever they'd agreed to. "I want you home. I need you in my arms, in my fucking bed—our bed. Make this quick, Madeline. My patience is thin. You're mine. You belong with me."

I felt a lump in my throat. Making him wait like this, not being able to come see me, check on me, it was asking a lot, and he was doing it because I'd asked.

"Thank you," I said softly, wishing I didn't have an audience.

"Don't thank me yet. I might still lose my fucking mind," he replied.

I laughed and held the phone tightly to my ear, wishing he were here with me. Wishing I didn't have to do this without him. But the man who had helped give me life and the one who was my life didn't need to be in the same room. It might explode.

"I love you," I said.

"You are my life," he replied.

I felt tears sting my eyes.

"He agreed to let you call me daily. He's using a goddamn burner phone, and it's untraceable. I can't track you. Know I'll move heaven and earth if you aren't delivered to me in three days."

I wiped at the tears that had rolled down my cheeks. "I will be."

I was trusting Liam, and Blaise was trusting me. I knew he didn't trust my father.

"When you return, if I've not uncovered the fucking traitor, we will have to face that. I need it handled. It's not safe for anyone here until it's handled. What you are asking of me puts my people in danger," Blaise said.

He didn't understand, and I couldn't tell him. Gina wasn't going to hurt any of them. She wasn't hurting me. She just wanted me gone.

"No one else is in danger. I would tell you if you were."

Blaise was silent a moment. I feared he had figured it out. My palms felt sweaty, and panic began to build in my chest. I hadn't been careful enough.

"Madeline, is it—"

"NO, Blaise. Do not ask me who. I've figured out some things, and we need to talk about it. Do not kill anyone. They don't deserve death."

He sighed heavily. "Fuck, the shit I do because you ask me to. At this rate, I'm going to be the worst damn boss in family history."

A laugh escaped me, and the pressure inside me lifted.

"I love you too," I replied.

Chapter TWENTY-SIX

BLAISE

I dropped my phone to the table and gripped the edges of it to calm my temper. Several deep breaths. I had to get control. She was alive, and although I didn't fucking like admitting it, Liam wasn't a danger to her. He was a danger to himself, however, because he had taken her from me.

Lifting my gaze, my eyes locked with Huck's.

"It was Gina," I told him, not needing confirmation from Madeline.

Her determination to protect who had helped Liam's men take her from me had made it real damn clear.

"Maddy confirmed it?" he asked, looking as sick as I felt.

I shook my head. "No. She won't tell me. Says she needs to explain to me why they did it. She thinks she caused it. Fucking blames herself for it. She's protecting her. If it were someone she didn't know or didn't trust, then she'd have told me. She doesn't want me killing Gina."

Huck let out a heavy sigh. "Garrett won't care what she says. He's gonna do what the hell he wants. You can't protect Gina from him. She's betrayed the family."

I nodded. I knew this, and as fucking furious as I was with Gina, Madeline didn't want her to die. It would destroy Madeline. How the hell did I keep this from happening? I wanted answers from Gina. I wanted to know why the fuck she'd done this, but if I asked and she admitted it, then she would be signing her death sentence. And I would be chancing Madeline never forgiving me.

"We say nothing for now," I told him.

Huck nodded, but I could see what I already knew in his eyes. There was no way to save Gina from this. She'd chosen to do it, and in doing so, she'd taken her own life.

"I take it, no one has hurt Maddy, if we aren't heading out on a killing spree," Huck said.

I let go of the table I was gripping and stood up.

We had checked into one of the hotels we owned in Miami moments before the call from Madeline came through. Huck had called off Gage, who would arrive here at any moment. I wasn't leaving because I knew there was nowhere else that Liam would have taken her. Until recently, his world was here. All his clubs, his filming studio, and his prostitute ring. The one place I couldn't locate was the damn MC headquarters. It was well hidden.

"She asked for three days," I told Huck. "She wants to know her father."

"We've watched him for weeks. He's shady as fuck with business, but so are we. I've not seen anything that tells us he's dirty," Huck said.

I nodded. "Yeah, I know. He's not going to hurt her. She wants to stay. I can't *not* let her have this. When she finds out I knew that her father was in Ocala and his exact location and didn't tell her"—I shook my head—"she's going to be fucking furious."

Huck shrugged. "She doesn't have to know."

I hadn't planned on telling her. My fear was that she'd figure it out on her own. Unless she was truly naive enough to believe I had just trusted a man with her safety and life after a five-minute phone conversation.

Chapter TWENTY-SEVEN

MADELINE

Sleep hadn't come easy last night. I had missed Blaise being beside me, the smell of him on the sheets, and sex. When I had fallen asleep, my dreams had been of him, and I'd woken up, aroused with no Blaise to fulfill me.

It wasn't until I stood up that the nausea came, and I spent some time over the toilet, then lying on the marble tiled floor with a cold cloth on my face. I knew I needed to eat something. A warm shower eased the tension from my shoulders, and I changed into the clothing Liam had brought in last night after the phone call with Blaise.

I didn't know what all had been said between the two men, but Liam seemed different. Today, I intended to ask my questions and start getting answers to my past.

Finding food first was on my list. If I didn't get some toast and maybe juice soon, the nausea would get worse.

The pair of jean shorts were loose on me and hung on my hips. The T-shirt fit better. It was cut for a woman and was black with *River Styx* on the front in glittery red letters.

I already knew this didn't represent the River Styx in Greek mythology. Last night, I'd heard Liam tell Micah to go there.

I was going to find out exactly what my father's motorcycle club did for a living. I had a feeling it wasn't exactly on the up-and-up.

Slipping my feet into the sandals with heels I had worn yesterday, I headed for the door. I had no idea where to find Liam, but I figured I would start at the library. I had only taken a few steps when a door to my left opened, and a barely dressed woman with dark brown hair and bigger boobs than I had ever seen in my life stepped out. Her gaze met mine, and she did a quick check of my clothing before smiling.

"Didn't know we had a new girl," she said. "Whose bed did you just crawl out of?" she asked with a smirk, nodding her head back at the door she'd just closed behind her. "I've had them all, but Tex is my favorite." She lowered her voice as she said it.

I opened my mouth to tell her that I hadn't crawled out of anyone's bed when another door opened behind us, and a blonde wearing a red halter top, a shiny white skirt that couldn't cover her butt completely, and a pair of stilettos walked out of a room. Her boobs were equally huge.

She looked from the brunette, then to me with a frown, then back to the brunette. "Who is she?"

"No clue. She was out here already when I came out of Tex's room," the brunette told her. She then looked back at me. "I'm Amethyst. This is Dylan," she told me before looking back at the blonde. "I thought you were done with Micah."

Dylan shrugged. "He was sweet last night."

Amethyst rolled her eyes. "Meaning he ate your pussy like a cat eating cream until you bounced on his dick."

The blonde flashed a smile. "He can eat pussy like no one else."

Amethyst shook her head and laughed. "I know. We all know. He eats them all."

Then, both females looked at me.

"What's your name?" Amethyst asked.

"Madeline," I replied. I started to tell them that Liam was my father, but Dylan gasped.

"You're Liam's girl!" She seemed surprised.

"No shit," Amethyst said, looking at me more closely now.

"Tell me, are you really fucking that hot Mafia boss? What's his name? He's a Hughes." Dylan bit her bottom lip, like she wanted details.

"Uh …" I started, but Amethyst held up her hand to stop me.

"Don't talk about it. Those bastards are fucked up. You want to live, you don't talk about them."

Who were these women?

"Besides, look at her. She's as sweet as a damn sugar cube. Those men fuck like animals. She would be broken if a Hughes fucked her," Amethyst said.

I fought the urge to put a hand protectively over my still-flat stomach. No need to draw attention there. At that moment, my stomach growled.

Both ladies looked at me.

"I'll show you to the kitchen on my way out. I'm sure one of the old ladies is already in there, cooking," she said.

That was a rude way to describe whoever was cooking for the people in this … club?

The two women in front of me had to be prostitutes. They looked the part, but I would admit they were much more attractive than I imagined real prostitutes to be. Kind of like *Pretty Woman*. Maybe that movie wasn't so far from reality as I had always thought.

"God, I hope it's Nina. She makes the best biscuits," Dylan said.

They began walking, so I decided if I wanted to eat, my best bet was to follow the two of them.

When we started down the stairs, Dylan glanced back at me. "I'm surprised Liam didn't post a guard at your door."

Frowning, I wondered if I needed one. Was there something to be afraid of here?

"The boys are going to salivate all over themselves," she added.

I looked at the way her body curved in the right places, and her breasts were spilling from the top she was wearing. "I think they've got plenty to look at around here already."

She laughed then, tossing her head back, as if I were a comedian. "You don't know much about men. Give them something sweet and innocent-looking with a face and body like yours, and they lose their damn minds," she said. "Sure, they fuck us and enjoy our performances at the club. We fulfill sexual fantasies for them, but we aren't innocent. We sure as hell don't look sweet. They can't teach us or own us."

I was stuck on performances. "What performances at the club?" I asked her.

Amethyst paused at the bottom step. "You know nothing about your daddy, do you?" she asked me.

"I'm here to fix that," I replied honestly.

She smiled at me. "We're strippers." She waved at Dylan. "And some of us also perform in adult movies. The Judgment owns five strip clubs, a film studio for the adult movies they produce, and a host of other things," she replied. "Your daddy is the president."

The president? Of strippers and adult movies, which I was going to assume meant porn. I should have asked more questions last night.

Did Blaise know this? God, I hoped he did and was okay with it. If he found this out after letting me stay, he might forget his promise not to kill people.

"I, uh, didn't know all that," I admitted.

She continued walking and I followed.

"Liam's gonna spank your ass for that," Dylan warned Amethyst.

"God, I hope he does," she replied. "Lately, he only lets Demi in his bed."

Dylan groaned. "He's gotta get bored with her eventually. Besides, she's almost, like, thirty. She's fucking old."

"Second-best thing is Micah." Amethyst paused then and looked at me. "Micah is the VP—vice president. So, fucking him ranks. He's had Dylan in and out of his bed for the past year."

So, that was what he had meant when he called Micah his VP last night.

I wanted to cover my ears. These women had to be around my age, and they had sex with my father? Surely not. Almost thirty? How old was he? At least forty? Micah was much younger. I understood that. But my father? Ewww.

"Kitchen is this way," Amethyst said as she walked down another long hallway.

They didn't speak until we reached a red door.

"I'm not eating, but I'm sure Dylan will join you. I've got to make sure my stomach is flat for tonight."

Dylan sighed as we walked into a big, bright kitchen. "It smells like fucking heaven," she called out.

The two women in the kitchen were not old. One might have been in her mid-thirties, but she was attractive. Dark blonde hair pulled up in a ponytail. Tight black shorts and a yellow halter top, tied just below her breasts. She was tanned and toned. The other lady, who looked up from the large pot she was stirring on the stove, had dark red hair cut into a bob, freckles. She was wearing a black tank top with a pair of white cutoff jean shorts that I could see some of her butt cheeks hanging out of. She might be thirty. Maybe. I saw no *old ladies* anywhere.

"Nina, you're a goddess," Dylan said, walking over to the blonde, who had just set down a pan of biscuits.

"If only all of us could eat like you and remain so thin," the woman she'd called Nina replied before looking at me, smiling. "And you must be Madeline. Lord, you're as gorgeous as Micah was carrying on about last night. Pres is gonna have his hands full with you around all these men."

Dylan reached for a biscuit and shot me a look. "Micah is a whore. Stay clear of him."

Nina looked at Dylan with a disgusted frown. "Says the girl who won't get out of his bed."

Dylan shrugged. "I said he was a whore. Not that I wasn't going to fuck him."

With a shake of her head, Nina looked back at me. "You are a vision, I swear to God."

"Thank you," I said, feeling embarrassed by the compliments.

"I'm Nina. My old man is Jars. He manages Strokes and didn't get in until an hour ago. You'll meet him later. This here"—she pointed to the redhead—"is Goldie. Her old man is Brick. You met him already."

Brick wasn't old either. I had a feeling the terms *old man* and *old lady* didn't mean actual age. I looked at Nina's hand and saw a tattoo ring around her ring finger. Did that mean she was married? Perhaps, in biker lingo, that was the meaning of it. Like an old ball and chain?

"These are the only two who have managed to claim one of The Judgment. They're hard to nail down. But it ain't stopping me from working on Micah," Dylan said.

Amethyst walked back into the room from the back and opened one of two large refrigerators and pulled out a bottle of water. "I've got to go," she said, then looked at Dylan. "And Micah don't want an old lady. You've got to let that shit go."

Dylan snarled at her as Amethyst left out the red door we had entered.

"It's true. He had one of those house whore's tits in his face as she bounced on his cock right there on the sofa last night, then went up to see Pres. When he came back down, he was going on about this pretty thing right here when that slutty Tracy bitch came up to him, topless, and asked him to fuck her ass. Which he did before he left."

Dylan scowled and stood up. "Ugh. No more," she said. "I need to go bleach my vagina."

"I agree!" Goldie called out as Dylan left behind Amethyst.

"Now, what can I get you to eat? It'll be a while before the boys all get down here. Long night," Nina said.

I wasn't sure I had much of an appetite anymore after all that information I had not wanted.

Had Micah actually done that to someone's butt in front of everyone?

"Try my cheese grits," Goldie told me, putting a spoonful of what she had been stirring in the pot on a plate. "Pres loves them," she assured me.

Nina took the plate from her and placed a biscuit on it. "I've not started the bacon or sausage yet. We were gonna do eggs next."

I was thankful they weren't doing the meat next. "This is good. I don't want any of the meat. Thank you."

"We got some jelly and butter for that biscuit, if you'd like. What about coffee?"

I felt bad, having them wait on me. I started to tell them I could fix it when the door opened behind me, and I turned to see Micah with disheveled hair, wearing a sleeveless white shirt and a pair of athletic shorts. He looked pissed until his gaze met mine, and then a slow grin spread across his face. I turned back to my plate of food. I didn't want to look at that man.

"Stop leering at her like she's your next meal," Nina scolded him.

"I'd die and go to heaven if she was," he drawled.

"You'd die all right, but it wouldn't be heaven you'd go to," Goldie called out from the stove, and then she winked at me.

"A taste of something that sweet, and eternity in hell would be worth it."

He was too close to me. Way too close.

"Back off." Nina waved a spatula at him. "Pres's daughter. DAUGHTER. Plus, her man almost killed off Butch and Grinder last night."

I lifted my head then. "It wasn't Blaise. It was one of his men," I told her, needing to defend him.

She shrugged. "Whoever it was, you are clearly important to the most dangerous bunch of fuckers I've ever heard of. No need to stir the nest."

"Look at her. I'm not violent, but I think I could become a killer myself if that was my hot piece of ass and someone took her from me," Micah said, pulling out the stool beside me and sitting down. "Tell me, sweet thing, does he eat that pussy properly?"

"For the love of God! Don't talk to her like that!" Nina yelled at him. "Dylan just left here. Go grab her if you woke up horny."

Micah brushed the hair on my shoulder back and leaned too close to me. I froze.

"She's just so damn pretty. All sweet and sexy," he said in a low voice as he moved closer to me.

"You got one fucking second to move away from my pregnant daughter before I put you down myself." Liam's voice was firm and loud, surprising not only me, but Nina and Goldie too.

Goldie gasped, and Nina squealed, dropping her spatula.

Micah moved away from me slowly then, and I let out the breath I'd been holding.

"Damn, smart motherfucker," Micah said, standing back up. "I'd have put my baby in her too."

"I'm not in the mood for this shit today," Liam said. "Why the hell are you up already?"

Micah shrugged. "Dylan slamming around when she left this morning woke me up."

Liam sighed. "Stop fucking her. She wants more than you're gonna give her."

Micah yawned and stretched, showing off his stomach before answering, "She keeps begging for my dick. I'm weak." Then, he looked at me and winked before walking over to the refrigerator.

I turned to Liam. "He told you last night," I said to him, realizing now that Liam's change in moods after talking to Blaise had been because he had been informed I was pregnant.

Liam nodded. "Yeah, he told me."

I was glad. Relieved. I hadn't wanted to tell him, but he needed to understand this was real. I wanted to be with Blaise. This wasn't a fling.

"I'm sorry, are you telling me that Blaise Hughes knocked you up?" Nina asked, her eyes wide.

A small smile touched my lips.

"Fuck yeah, he did. Look at her. He's powerful because he makes the right damn moves. That is a move I can respect," Micah said before taking a half-gallon of orange juice from the fridge and drinking from the container.

"Micah." Liam's tone was another warning.

Nina looked nervous as she looked at Liam. "Is it safe? He's ..." She paused and glanced at me briefly. "I don't want anyone to die."

I realized what she was asking. I liked Nina. I didn't want her or Goldie or any of the other women to worry. I knew what it felt like, fearing that the man you loved might get hurt or not come back from something. I lived it.

"I spoke with Blaise last night. He's not going to do anything. I want to be here. To get to know Liam," I assured her.

She didn't look convinced. She fisted a towel in her hand as she looked at me. "You seem like a real sweet girl. It's hard to imagine you living among those people. I'd be terrified that I would make a wrong move, and a bullet between my eyes would be the result. I just can't imagine that a Hughes would be okay with not only their woman, but the woman carrying their child and heir to be somewhere they can't get to them."

I wasn't going to correct her. The family was feared, and I knew that needed to remain if they were to keep their power. I knew a side of Blaise they didn't, and I wasn't going to share it with anyone. They could be terrified of him. He would want that. I didn't need to keep defending him.

"Three days is all I have. If I'm not returned, then, yes, you should all be worried," I replied.

Nina took a deep breath. "I say we make it two. Just in case those crazy bastards change their minds," she said.

Liam didn't respond. Micah, however, grinned like he was up for a challenge. That man was danger. One day, he was going to say the wrong thing to the wrong woman.

"I think she might just be worth the fight," Micah said.

"Pregnant!" Nina reminded him.

He shrugged. "I could overlook that."

"Jesus Christ," Liam muttered. "Nina, could you or Goldie bring breakfast to the library? If I don't get Madeline away from Micah, I'm going to lose my shit."

Taking my plate, I stood up, wanting to get away from him too. I didn't want to argue about that. The sooner I got Liam away from everyone else, the sooner I could ask questions.

Chapter TWENTY-EIGHT

BLAISE

"You aren't going to make it three days," Gage said, standing at the tall windows of the penthouse, looking out at the ocean.

Did he think I didn't fucking know that?

I walked over to the bar to pour another drink. I needed to hear her voice. I needed to see her face and feel her in my arms. Last night, I hadn't even been able to lie in the motherfucking bed.

"We can just go take her," Gage suggested.

Growling, I glared at the glass in front of me. "No, we can't. I promised her. I have to let her do this."

Gage shrugged his arms, then turned to look at me. "Then, we need to get you some fucking Valium."

I slugged back the drink and slammed the glass back down on the bar. "Won't help," I ground out. "Nothing but having her back will help."

"We going to let him live once we get her back?" Gage asked. He was always so damn bloodthirsty.

"She'd never forgive me if we killed him. He's safe. The whole fucking club is safe," I said angrily. "Unless they touch her."

My phone rang, and I jerked it up, seeing Levi's name on the screen.

"Gina vanished," he said. "Angel is at Garrett's, but Gina isn't."

I was torn between vengeance and relief. I didn't think I could forgive her enough to let her live, but, damn, she had been like a sister once. If she was gone, I didn't have to make a choice.

"Then, she's gone. No one looks for her," I told him.

"You sure?" Levi asked.

"When Garrett finds out that she handed Madeline over, she's dead. Unless she's leaves and can become invisible," I told him.

"Okay," he replied. "I'll be there in a few hours. Heading out to the plane now."

I ended the call and put the phone down on the table.

"She ran," Gage said simply.

I nodded.

"Cameras didn't get anything?" he asked.

I hadn't asked for details, but then I wasn't positive that Levi hadn't helped her. I'd never ask him. That ended here. It was done.

I shrugged. "Does it matter?"

I lifted my gaze to meet his. He understood my meaning.

Madeline thought Gina had had a reason to hand her over like she had, but no reason would be good enough.

Gina hadn't been certain Madeline would be safe with Liam. I hadn't even been fucking sure, and I'd been stalking the bastard for weeks. I'd had a plan. When I was positive that Liam meant her no harm, I would have been with her and had my men there, too, when she met the man who had played a hand in her existence. What Gina had chosen was unforgivable. She had known it, and she'd left before she paid for it.

Huck walked into the room with Chinese takeout he'd gone to get. "How much longer do we wait for Maddy to call before we move?"

"She didn't give me a time. Just today," I replied.

Huck walked over and put a box in front of me. "Kung pao. You need to eat," he said, then went to the table with the rest.

"I need to fucking eat," Gage informed him. "Did you get my General Tso's?"

Huck shoved a box across the table. "I got your damn spring rolls, too, but I ate one on the way back and the other in the elevator."

Gage scowled. "So, you ate them both?"

Huck nodded and sat down. "Sure did. Go get your own damn food."

I looked down at the box and knew I had to eat. Especially if I wasn't going to be able to sleep. When it was time to go get her, I didn't need to be weak.

Chapter TWENTY-NINE

MADELINE

During breakfast, Brick had come in, followed by Tex. Then, Liam excused himself to go deal with some issue on set. From what Tex had told him, their most popular actress was angry with the guy she was supposed to have sex with. Although he was trying to filter his words, I was aware that my father's club also produced porn, thanks to Amethyst. I hadn't mentioned it though.

When Liam returned to the library, I had started to doze off on the sofa. Quickly, I sat up, ready to get some questions answered. He sighed and sank down onto the sofa across from mine. I wondered how much of this he enjoyed.

"Sorry about that," he said with a half-smile.

"I imagine dealing with actresses of the nude variety can have a lot of drama," I replied.

He let out a chuckle and rubbed his bearded chin. "That one didn't get by you," he said.

"Your club deals in sex. It's better than drugs," I replied honestly.

He nodded. "Yeah, I think so. There isn't as much of the violence that comes with the other."

"How did you meet my mother?" I asked him before another interruption could come in the door.

"Those damn horse races she loved so much. Not sure what all you've been told, but part of it, I imagine, was true.

"Her father, Eli, had pissed off someone in our organization and killed one of our men. I won't get into details because truth is, neither side was right. My job was to find Etta, seduce her, and then take her. So, I went looking for her."

He smiled then and shook his head. "Damn if she wasn't the one to seduce me. I had been warned about her beauty. That was one reason I was chosen because, believe it or not, I was considered attractive. I didn't struggle with the ladies. And my dad was the boss."

I laughed then. He was still a handsome man, and I had no doubt he had been a head-turner when he was younger.

"Etta was full of fire. She wasn't afraid of anything. Nothing was impossible to her. She was a force, and I was instantly drawn to her. Sure, I kept my head about me for the first few days, but she made me forget what the fuck I was supposed to be doing. That girl had me forgetting who I was with one of those sweet smiles of hers.

"I knew I had to protect her, but I wasn't sure how to do it without getting us both killed. She didn't know who I was. I didn't tell her. I was afraid to. I knew who she was, and she had been honest with me from the beginning. Warning me who her father was. She made me chase after her, telling me that she was afraid for my safety. I told her we could be secret about it, and for a short moment in time, I had all I'd ever wanted.

"Etta became my world. I was ready to move heaven and earth to have her. I thought of going to her father and telling him I needed help getting free of the life I'd been born into. I wasn't just a member of the gang, I would be expected to take over after my father. I was willing to be a soldier for the family, go into the shit no one wanted to deal with—whatever he wanted from me if I could just have Etta."

Liam sighed and rubbed his forehead, as if retelling this was difficult.

"I never got that chance. I'd underestimated Eli, and that was a mistake. He had a closer eye on Etta than I'd realized. Than she even realized. She was told who I was and why I'd been at the track. That she was my mark. That she was going to be used as revenge for the death of one of our guys."

Liam crossed his arms over his broad chest and sighed.

"Young love in a fucking world of monsters. I only know what I've told you because I spent years searching for her. It wasn't until she'd been gone for five years and the gang that I belonged to had dissolved in their own internal war that I met a guy whose name I won't repeat. He was part of the family. He was who informed me that Etta had been pregnant with my kid when she ran and they'd never been able to find her. Goddammit, I'd thought losing her had hurt. But knowing I'd lost my kid too ..." He pressed his lips together. "I became a man possessed, looking for her, for you. But nothing. She had left no trace.

"It wasn't until six weeks ago that I finally got some relevant info. One of my guys who manages one of the strip clubs heard another organization in there, talking about the fact that Blaise Hughes had a weakness. The monster had fallen in love. He'd already killed five men who had tried abducting her."

"It was two," I told him.

Liam smirked. "No, sweetheart, it was five. The two that his boys had taken out when they rescued you hadn't acted alone. They worked under someone, who worked under someone. Hughes walked his arrogant ass into their places of business and put bullets in every one of their heads.

"You think you know him, but you know the man that loves you. I heard him on that phone. He was a man who would raise every hell on earth to get back the woman he loved. But you need to understand. The gentleness he offers you is singular. He is known for his brutality. He is feared for it. Don't ever forget that."

I sat there as Liam's words sank in. Blaise had never told me he'd gone after and killed other men involved with my abduction. What else did I not know? The man Liam was talking about didn't sound like the man I knew. Sure, Blaise had killed and I knew he had a dark side but he wasn't cruel.

"I didn't see how Hughes having a weakness affected me or this club. But then my man went on to say that Blaise had been stalking her for years, making sure she was safe. That she was the granddaughter of a former boss and her mother had died when she was only three. But when her father tried to sell her for money, Blaise put her father and her brother down." Liam held my gaze then, and I saw emotion in them that made a lump form in my throat. "There hadn't been a Hughes granddaughter in over eighty years. Besides, if Blaise was in love with her then she wasn't his blood relation. What I did know was that there had been a boss who had filled in for Garrett Hughes until he came of age, and that man had a daughter.

"My fucking heart broke in that moment when I realized Etta was dead. But it was also healed because she had given me a daughter. One exactly like her mother if she had managed to reel in the fucking Devil himself. I started searching then, asking questions. I got pictures, and the moment I saw you, I knew. You were Etta's, but you were also mine. Because although you have her beauty, that smile is mine."

I sat back, wrapping my arms around my waist as I thought about all he'd lost and gone through. He hadn't abandoned my mother. She had died, thinking he was a danger to us. My chest ached that she never knew how much he had loved her. That she had settled for someone like Luke when she could have had Liam. I could have been raised with a real father.

"He isn't the Devil," I said finally, not wanting the man who should have raised me to think of the man I loved in such a negative way.

Liam gave me a sad smile. "Yes, he is. But now that I've spoken to him, I don't think there is another human alive who could give you the world while keeping you safe the way he can. Yes, I was able to take you out from under his nose, but that was because Tex had worked his magic on that Gina woman. We had watched until we found a weak link. Gina was more than willing to offer you up and do it so that you weren't harmed. I don't know why she did it, and I do hope she doesn't die for it."

I shook my head. "She won't. I think I understand why she did, and I won't let them kill her," I said with conviction.

Liam chuckled. "I'm willing to bet you can do just that too. Before I'd heard how insane Hughes sounded over you on the phone, I wouldn't have thought you could. But that man's weakness seems to truly be in the form of my daughter"—he nodded his head toward my stomach—"and my grandchild."

"I won't let you hurt him," I warned Liam.

If there was a side to pick and I was forced, I would choose Blaise. He needed to know that.

Liam laughed. "I risked my life when I had them take you. I wasn't sure I'd see another birthday, but I wanted to know my daughter. I'd lived this shit life without Etta, and by God, if there was a part of her—of us—walking this earth, then I was willing to risk it to meet you. You don't hurt the Devil, Madeline. The Devil destroys you."

I scowled, not liking Blaise being referred to as the Devil.

Liam just shook his head with amusement twinkling in his eyes. "You'll see one day. I'm not lying about your man. I'm telling you the truth because if that is the world you want to live in, then you need to know. Those enemies of his I warned you about? They're stupid fuckers who think they can beat him. They'll all die, trying. Hundreds already have. I thought I could keep you here, offer you a more average life. A good life. But I saw your face on the phone when you spoke to him, and I heard the agony in his voice when I spoke to him. I understand that kind of love, but I wasn't as powerful as he is. I wasn't able to keep mine."

Hundreds? No, that was an exaggeration.

Liam leaned forward, holding out a phone to me. "Call him before he snaps and comes after more of my men."

I took the phone and realized this phone was different than the last one he gave me. Blaise had known they'd change out their phones, but I doubted he was ever wrong. I dialed his number.

"Madeline." He said my name before the first ring finished.

"Yes," I replied, unable not to smile at the sound of his voice.

"Are you okay? Feel okay? Have you been sick? I'm ready for you to come home. I can't do two more days."

I pressed my lips together to keep from laughing at the urgency in his voice. This was not a monster or the Devil. Liam had bought into the lies that the family, I was sure, had created. The more powerful they seemed, the safer they were.

"I'm good. I got a little sick this morning, but I had a delicious breakfast. I miss you too," I told him.

"Let me get you today," he pleaded.

I looked across at my father and decided it was time to play my hand. "I'll come back to you today, if you allow me to see Liam whenever I want to. I understand safety. You can decide how that is done, but if I walk out of here today, I want to know I can see him again."

Liam was watching me with interest.

"Fuck," Blaise muttered. "I was expecting this. I want you here. I'll do whatever the hell you want from me. But he's got to swear that he contacts you through me."

"No. He's my father, and I don't want you to control that. You can't control everything in my life, Blaise," I said angrily. "I am not a child. He isn't going to hurt me. If he had planned on it, wouldn't he have done so by now?"

Liam covered his mouth with one hand but I could see the smile in his eyes.

"Fine. Fuck, fine. But if this puts you in harm's way, I will kill every motherfucker remotely connected to that damn club," Blaise replied with a deadly calm.

"You won't have to kill anyone. Liam wants me safe too," I told him gently.

"Just let me come get you," Blaise said.

I looked at Liam. "Can he come here to get me, or would you rather take me to him?"

Liam held out his hand for the phone. I handed it over.

"Hughes," he said. "If I let you come here, I am placing my entire club in danger. So, understand this is me telling you that I intend to make sure Madeline is safe. I want my daughter and grandchild to be free to come see me. If that means the Devil has to come with them, then so fucking be it. As long as you would die for the both of them. That's all I ask."

He listened, and then I saw a smile tug at his lips.

"I will text you the address from my personal phone."

He held the phone back out to me.

"We might be one big, happy family before it's all over," Liam said.

I cradled the phone to my ear. "Hey."

"Have him send the damn address now. I'm coming to get you."

"But what did you say to his offer?" I asked.

He sighed. "Madeline, what do you think I said? If having that man in your life makes you happy, then I'm gonna fucking do it. I don't have to like it, but I will do it."

I smiled as tears stung my eyes. "Thank you."

"Just get that fucker to send me the address. I need you."

Chapter THIRTY

MADELINE

Three black SUVs pulled up outside as I stood beside Liam, waiting on Blaise.

"How many people did he bring?" Liam muttered.

The middle SUV's passenger door swung open, and when I saw his black boots hit the pavement, I went running to him. Blaise took three long strides and grabbed me as I threw myself into his arms. I let out a sob as his smell and warmth filled me. He buried his head in the crook of my neck and inhaled deeply.

"I missed you," I told him.

He took a deep breath and held me tighter. "I don't think I have words for the hell I've just lived through," he finally said before pulling back and holding my face in his hands. He searched me, as if he was sure he'd see a mark or a scratch.

"I'm fine. I promise," I assured him.

He pressed a kiss to my lips before finally lifting his gaze and looking back over my shoulder at Liam. He nodded his head once, then pulled me to his side before walking toward my father. I saw Micah standing outside now beside Liam, and I prayed silently to a god I wasn't sure existed that he didn't say anything stupid to upset Blaise.

"Can't say I ever thought the day would come when I willingly let you walk into my sanctuary," Liam said as we approached. Then, his eyes went to me. "But seems we never expected to love the same woman. Differently, of course."

"You could have come to me. Asked. Instead of taking her." Blaise's tone wasn't friendly, and I realized I was going to need to step in.

"And I'm sure you would have shared a beer with me and we'd have chatted like old friends," Liam drawled.

I put my hand on Blaise's chest. "Be nice. He's apologized for the way it was handled."

Blaise looked down at me, and the steely look in his eyes softened.

"I don't know what the right way would have been, but there had to have been a better one than what I chose. I wanted to know my daughter, and until I spent time with her, I wasn't sure she was safe. With you. I had only heard that Blaise Hughes had a woman. I didn't know how important she was to you until I spoke to her and, of course, you."

Blaise's hand tightened on my side. "She wants to know you, then she can know you. That doesn't mean I let my guard down."

Liam nodded. "I understand." He motioned to Micah. "This is Micah Abe. My VP."

Blaise cut his eyes to Micah, and I held my breath.

Micah, however, wasn't like the guy I'd been around earlier. He wasn't smiling. He simply nodded his head at Blaise and said nothing. I let out a relieved sigh.

"She has your number when she's ready to see you. We need to go," Blaise said to Liam.

I tried to step forward, and Blaise's hand tightened on my waist.

I glared up at him. "Let me tell him goodbye," I said through clenched teeth.

Blaise's nostrils flared like they did when he was controlling himself. "Tell him from here."

I pushed my fingernail into his chest. "Back off and let me do this my way. He's my father, Blaise. He trusted you to come here. Now, stop it."

Blaise took a deep breath, and his hand finally released me. I gave him a grateful smile, then stepped forward to Liam. I felt awkward now, but I had to do this. Our time had been short, but I had a promise of more.

When Liam opened his arms for me to step into for a hug, I went willingly and tried very hard not to let my emotions get the best of me.

"Thank you," I whispered.

"I'm here. Always. Don't be a stranger," he replied.

"I won't. I promise," I told him.

Then, I stepped back, and he let me go. Blaise's hand was on my waist immediately. I rolled my eyes at Liam, who looked like he was fighting not to laugh. Then, I waved one last time and turned with Blaise to walk away. Back to the life I belonged in.

Chapter THIRTY-ONE

LIAM

"She doesn't have a fucking clue, does she?" Micah whispered beside me. The note of awe in his voice was understandable.

"Nope. I tried to warn her, but she refuses to believe anything bad about him," I told Micah.

"She just poked his chest with her fingernail and scolded his ass in front of us," Micah said. "And the bastard didn't flinch. He took it. She won," he said, shaking his head. "Damn, she's a badass."

I chuckled. "No. She is in love with a man we don't know. I doubt anyone does. He will go out tomorrow and probably blow some motherfucker's head off, but she won't know it. She'd never believe it."

I watched as the daughter I'd thought I'd never know punched a massive man holding the door open for her in the arm and said something to him with the same sass I remembered in her mother. She trusted the monsters that were known as The Family, and it was clear they adored her.

Damn, Etta would be proud of her. My throat burned as I thought of the fact that she was missing it all. She deserved this. She'd have been a damn good mother.

"Do you trust him?" Micah asked me.

"With my daughter, yes."

He sighed. "What about us?"

I glanced over at Micah. "Because of her, we're safe. Well, I am. If you open your damn mouth and piss him off, I don't think you're safe. In fact, I'm not sure Madeline likes you much. Walk the line, son," I told him and turned back to watch the black SUVs drive away.

She'd come back to visit. I knew this wasn't goodbye. But it still made my chest ache to see her go so quickly.

"Does she know he killed nine men for her?" he asked me.

I shrugged. "She thought his men had killed two. I told her it was five, that he had gone after the others."

Micah laughed. "So, she thinks he killed three?"

"I wasn't sure she could handle the truth or if she'd even believe me."

Micah nodded. "Yeah, it's hard to believe one man could walk into a meeting and take out nine armed men alone, then walk out like nothing had happened. Word was, he'd used a silencer, and no one knew they were all dead in there until hours later, when they hadn't come out."

"I tried to tell her he was the Devil, and she got pissed." I chuckled. As if I had come up with that name for him.

"Fucker is obsessed with her," Micah said.

"He really is," I agreed.

Micah sighed then. "I'd been willing to face your wrath for her, but I'm gonna choose life and let that one go."

I laughed loudly as we walked back into the house. One thing that Blaise Hughes was good for, for sure, was keeping my whore of a VP away from my daughter.

"Damn, it's a shame though," he muttered. "Women like that don't come around often."

Damn if I didn't know it. No one had ever been like Etta. I'd live this life with a void that could never be filled.

Chapter THIRTY-TWO

MADELINE

Blaise held me against him the entire ride to the private airport. He said little, and I left him alone with his thoughts. I knew seeing me touch Liam and being that close to other men had been hard for him. He needed to work through it because I intended to see my father again.

I turned my face to his chest and took a deep breath. I loved his smell. It made everything that had been wrong right. I moved to place a hand on his chest, but his fingers wrapped around my wrist.

Lifting my face to look up at him, I saw his jaw working. "What's wrong?" I asked him, now worried that there was something I had missed.

I was so happy to be back with him that I hadn't realized he wasn't feeling it the way I was.

"Huck is driving," he said through clenched teeth. "We aren't alone."

I frowned. "I don't understand."

Blaise looked down at me. His eyes full of something that made the area between my legs tingle. "I won't fuck you with an audience. No one sees or hears your pleasure but me."

I bit my bottom lip, and his eyes flared with a hunger that excited me.

"The plane," I told him.

He didn't say anything as his fingers tightened their grip on my wrist until it was almost painful. "Not sure I can make it that long," he bit out.

This was hot. He was struggling with it, and that made me ache. I squirmed in my seat, trying to find some release. His hand moved to my thigh and held me still.

"Don't," he warned.

I wanted to whimper, but the look in his eyes kept me silent. I stared up at him, biting my bottom lip, unsure I could wait now. This was his fault. He was the one who had gotten me worked up.

He shoved my legs open, uncrossing them. "Don't look back here," he growled out at Huck. Then, his other hand covered my mouth.

Blaise shoved my sundress up and jerked the crotch of my panties over, then pushed two fingers inside of me. My eyes rolled back in my head, and my moan was muffled by his large hand.

He bent his head down until his lips were on my ear. "My pussy." His claim sounded angry.

I wasn't going to argue. He pumped the two fingers in and out of me, and I moved the leg closest to him over his lap to open myself wider.

"You keep that shit up, and I'm going to fuck you in this backseat, then kill Huck because he heard you scream out in pleasure."

I knew he wasn't going to kill his friend, but it still made me afraid to push him.

"Sweet pussy juices are running down my hand," he groaned, making me shiver. "I'm going to bury my face between these thighs and eat you until you are begging me to stop."

Yes. That. I wanted that.

Lifting my hips to his hand, I moaned again, and his hand pressed harder against my mouth. He shook his head at me in warning. If he wanted me to calm down, then he needed to stop talking dirty. It was driving me crazy.

"If any of them touched you, I'll have to kill them." It didn't sound like a threat. He said it as calmly as if he were telling me a fact.

My father's words that Blaise was evil and the Devil began to come back to me. Haunting me while I still drove closer to the orgasm my body was craving. I wasn't sure I cared at that moment. No one had touched me. They were safe.

"Pull over," Blaise shouted at Huck.

The SUV turned and went for a few more minutes before it stopped, and Huck all but jumped out and closed the door behind him.

Blaise's hand was gone, and I cried out at the absence of his touch. His eyes burned bright, and I watched him unfasten his jeans and jerk them down with his briefs in one tug.

"Lie back and open those pretty legs," he ordered.

I scooted back and did as I had been told. Then, he grabbed my left leg and pulled it up and over his shoulder as he shoved inside of me, making me cry out in pleasure-pain.

"FUCK!" he growled, and his face looked like a man who had lost all control.

He began slamming into me over and over as I lifted my hips to meet each thrust.

"Did anyone touch you?" he shouted.

I shook my head.

"No one put their hands on what is mine?" he asked me again.

"NO!" I screamed.

He leaned down as his pumping slowed and ran a finger over my bottom lip. I smelled my arousal on him.

"No one had better ever touch you. Do you understand? When it comes to you, nothing else fucking matters," he whispered.

I nodded frantically, needing him to start moving again. I lifted my hips, and Blaise grabbed my leg and jerked it up higher as he began thrusting into me again. My back arched off the seat as I cried out.

I had feared I was twisted and dark because I had loved him even when I thought he had killed my family. But I knew I was those things now because his threats and the dangerous gleam in his eyes as he was fucking me had turned my arousal up, making my pleasure skyrocket. I was getting off on his power.

When had I become so messed up in the head?

"That's it. Squeeze my dick with that tight pussy. Fuck me until I don't want to go kill some son of a bitch because you were taken from me." His voice was low as he spoke.

I looked up at him, and those green eyes resembled a storm about to cause destruction.

"I'm going to fill you up with cum now and in the fucking plane, then shoot it all over your tits and ass when we get home. I want you covered in me. FUCKING MINE! *No one* takes what is mine!"

His words sent me into a spiral, and my orgasm exploded. The world around me faded away as I rode it, gasping for air.

Yes, I was definitely twisted in the head.

Chapter THIRTY-THREE

MADELINE

The house was quiet when I came upstairs for breakfast. Blaise had already left the bed. I pulled the black belt on my robe tighter as I walked through the house toward the kitchen. The smell of coffee was all that hit me when I entered the room. Blaise was sitting at the table with a cup in his hand and the phone to his ear. His eyes met mine, and they softened.

"Let me know what they say," he said into the phone, then ended the call and put it on the table, never breaking eye contact with me.

"Where is everyone?" I asked him, glancing at the clock to see it was only eight in the morning.

"Gone. Everyone is gone. They're relocating," he replied, then stood up.

"Relocating?" I asked, confused.

Blaise walked toward me and nodded his head.

"Where?"

I wanted more answers. He, however, was looking at me like he intended to have me for breakfast.

"Temporarily, they're moving to other properties I own. Except Angel. She's moving into Garrett's," Blaise replied as he took the belt I had tied tightly and used it to pull me to him.

He buried his face in my hair and sighed, causing me to shiver.

"Why are they temporarily moving?" I asked him, afraid he was about to distract me.

"Because we're staying here alone until our house is ready. Then, we will move into it, and the guys can move back here." Blaise said, then began a trail of soft kisses from my temple down to my neck.

My hand went up to touch his hair as he bent down over my shoulder and took a gentle nibble.

"Our house? Where is our house?" I asked breathlessly.

Blaise tugged on the belt hard one more time until it came loose and fell open. "It's on Hughes Farm property, but set back farther from the big house. You can't see it unless you drive back there," he replied, then continued his trail of kisses until he was at the top of my left breast.

I was losing focus.

"Wait. Stop. Tell me what is happening first," I said, although I didn't sound very sincere about the stopping part as my hands fisted in his hair.

Blaise lifted his head up, then licked at my nipple while looking at me. He stood up then, and his hands took my waist, and he placed me on the island behind me so that we were eye-level. "Well, baby, I'm about to lay you back and eat your pussy because I'm hungry and you look really fucking sweet."

A small laugh escaped me, and I felt my nipples harden to the point of sharp pain. "That's not what I meant," I replied, and he ran his thumb over my chin.

"Hmm, okay," he said in a husky whisper. "I'm done sharing you. This, us, it's forever. My baby is inside you. I want a home with just us. Somewhere that I will know you are always safe. I don't want motherfuckers in my kitchen in the morning when you come walking in, looking like this. I want just us. That's what is happening," he told me.

His hands slid up the insides of my thighs.

"We are moving? You don't want to stay here?" I asked him, afraid he was giving up somewhere he loved because he was concerned about me being safe.

His hands stopped just as his fingers were about to find out I hadn't put on panties. I looked into his eyes, and although I was sitting, the way he was looking at me made my knees feel weak. I got butterflies in my stomach.

"You deserve a big motherfucking house that you can decorate just the way you want it. I used to watch you struggle to just make it to the next day, and I'd wish like hell I could take you away. Give you the world. I can now," he said and moved his hands up one more inch. His eyes turned darker as he felt the dampness, telling him I was aroused with nothing to cover it. "My pussy is bare." His voice was a low rumble.

I nodded but reached up to grab his face with my hands. We weren't through with this conversation.

"I don't want you giving up your home because you think I need some fancy house that I can decorate," I told him.

Blaise shoved my legs open as his gaze grew darker. "You are my fucking home, Madeline. You. Not this house. You," he said, then ran his finger over my swollen clit.

I whimpered. I wanted that to be true. I wanted to be his home because there was no doubt in my mind that he was mine. Even with the bad things he had done, I wanted him.

"When you were gone, so was my fucking soul. I live for you now," he said, then thrust two fingers inside me.

My hands moved from his face to his shoulders as I gasped.

"And this. Your pretty face keeps me human, your sweet smile calms my rage, your smart mouth keeps me sane, and this hot little pussy owns me."

While that wasn't Shakespeare, it was pretty poetic, coming from a man who killed people regularly.

"I love you," I said as he began to slide his fingers in and out of me.

"I thought I loved you," he whispered. "But I'm well fucking beyond that now. I worship you. Fucking adore you. Now, lie back like a good girl so I can lick this needy pussy."

I didn't say anything else. I wasn't sure there was anything else to say.

Lying back, I watched as Blaise unzipped his pants and shoved them down, freeing his erection before he grabbed my legs and put them over his shoulders. As his head lowered, every nerve in my body felt as if it were sizzling. At the first touch of his tongue, I cried out his name and grabbed his head. He flicked at my sensitive clit several times, then tasted me like I was in fact his meal. My body trembled as it climbed toward the sweet ecstasy that I knew would come.

"Blaise …" I moaned his name, loving the sound of it.

He tilted his head back so that he could see my face as he continued to drive me wild with his mouth. The lust swirling in his eyes was exciting and wicked. I loved when he looked at me like that. I wanted to do everything he asked of me. Not because I had to in order to make him happy, but because his pleasure was mine.

His tongue curled up after one last lick. "When you come, I want it on my dick," he said as he stood up and moved me so that he could slide inside me easily.

Each of his hands grabbed my ass and jerked me up against him, and he sank deeper inside me.

"I swear if I could just keep you here like this all the time, I fucking would," he groaned.

I wrapped my arms around his neck as he began rocking inside of me. He didn't go fast, but instead took his time. Driving us both crazy as our climax built slowly. He bit the curve between my neck and shoulder, and I let out a sharp cry as he sank his teeth in. It hurt, but somehow, it also sent jolts directly to my center.

Blaise lifted his head with a sinful grin on his face. "Fuck, I like biting you," he said in a deep voice.

The coiling promise of euphoria tightened between my legs, and as it slammed into me, I grabbed Blaise's shoulders. My body jerked against him as I cried out. Blaise's shout came almost immediately after, and I felt the warmth of his release spill into me. His hips lurched forward, and a tremor ran over his body.

I wrapped my arms around him and laid my cheek against his chest. He pulled me closer, holding me. We stayed that way as our pulses slowed and our bodies relaxed. I was sure I had a mark on my neck again, but I didn't care. If that got him off, biting me like an animal, then I liked it.

"Sometimes, I fear I'm going to fuck you to death," he said near my ear, and I laughed.

Pulling back, I looked at him. "There are worse ways to go," I teased.

He smirked and then pulled out of me while keeping his eyes on my entrance. His depraved need to see his semen leak out of me was also something I liked. If that did it for him, then he could do it every time.

When his eyes lifted to meet mine, I saw the territorial gleam in them.

"Yes, I'm yours," I told him.

It seemed to ease the monster inside him.

Chapter THIRTY-FOUR

BLAISE

Huck was standing outside the black SUV he drove with his arms crossed over his chest and the metal flashing at his hip. I glanced back at the door to make sure Madeline hadn't followed me. She had been running her bath water when Huck called me to tell me he was outside.

The intensity of his expression told me this was serious. He reached for the handle of the door and paused a moment, but said nothing before opening it. Sitting in the backseat was Gina. Gagged with her wrists and ankles tied with a rope. Her eyes were red and swollen from crying. I could see her begging me not to kill her, although she wasn't fighting to scream or speak through the gag.

"Didn't want anyone to know. Just in case," Huck said.

I knew what he meant. If I didn't want her dead, Garrett couldn't know we had her, or he'd kill her himself. There was a difference between my father and me. One I feared would make me a weaker boss. Killing a man I knew deserved it was easy. I had no remorse. I did it more often than I ever wanted

Madeline to know. If she looked at me differently, I wasn't sure I could survive that.

My father would have seen Gina sitting in this seat and pulled out his Glock, pointed it at her head, killed her, and walked away, ordering Huck to clean it up. But I couldn't do that. I paused. I didn't even think to go for the gun on my hip. Instead, I studied her as Madeline's words went through my head. She wouldn't admit it was Gina, but she truly believed that Gina had had a reason. Nothing was Madeline's fault. That shit was something she'd drummed up in her head. She took blame for bullshit she shouldn't. She had done it as long as I had been watching her.

"You said to let her stay gone, but she came to me. I didn't go looking," Huck said.

I nodded. I'd figured as much. "Where did she find you?"

"I was coming out of Devil's, and she was standing by the car. Said she wanted to talk to you. Explain," he said.

"That was a bad move," I told her. "If you'd stayed gone, you could have lived."

She trembled, and tears filled her eyes again. I couldn't take the gag out and let her talk. Madeline could hear her if she screamed. I wasn't sure Madeline needed to know we had found her. Garrett was going to order this kill if he didn't do it himself. Madeline couldn't handle this shit. She'd think it was her fault. Blame Gina's stupidity on herself. I would not let Madeline hold that kind of thing on her shoulders. I wanted her happy. I wanted to be the one to give her fucking joy. Make her smile. Not destroy her.

"You took what was mine. Gave her to fucking strangers who you couldn't be sure wouldn't hurt her. You TOOK her from me." I felt my temper starting to build. Remembering how fucking terrified I'd been when I found Madeline gone.

"Even if I let you live because Madeline begged me to and still refuses to tell me it was you, Garrett won't. You know that."

Gina jerked and winced, as if I had slapped her. If Garrett didn't take the shot, he'd order one of the men to take it. This was prolonged torture for her. She had to know she wouldn't get a chance to explain. There was no explanation that would save her.

"Take the gag off her." Madeline's voice came from behind me.

FUCK.

My chest burned with regret as I turned to see her wrapped in her black robe, standing a few feet behind us.

She was so naive. So damn sweet. I was going to end up breaking her. This life I led would show her enough damn shit to crush her.

"Madeline," I warned, "go back inside."

She glared at me and shook her head. "Take the gag off. She should get a chance to talk. Besides, just because she ran doesn't mean that she did it. I haven't told you who handed me over to Tex and Brick. You have no proof."

Her chin was tilted up defiantly, and she looked so goddamn cute that I wanted to take her inside and tie her ass up. Keep her away from this part of my life.

"We know she did it. You don't have a poker face, baby," I replied.

Madeline's gaze narrowed. "Take the fucking gag off her, Blaise!"

Huck cleared his throat, and I swore to God, if the fucker laughed, I was going to punch him in that smug face of his. I swung my gaze from Madeline to Huck and shot him a warning look. I could think she was cute as fuck, trying to be a badass, but no one else got to enjoy it.

I moved toward Gina, whose eyes went wide, and she looked down at the gun on my hip. She thought I was about to take her out now. Little did she realize, I was fucking owned by the blonde behind me, calling the damn shots. If she'd known how deep my obsession was with Madeline, she wouldn't have been brave enough to take her from me.

I jerked the gag off with more force than necessary and grabbed her face in my hand and squeezed it so tightly that I knew it would bruise. The demons inside me that wanted to make her pay for touching Madeline, for giving her to fucking strangers, were in control. It was hard to rein that in.

Gina whimpered.

"BLAISE! Let her go!" Madeline yelled from behind me.

I slowly eased my grip on her face and took a deep breath, trying to calm down. "She's the only fucking reason I've not killed you," I said in a low voice, then shoved her face away as I let go of it.

When I backed up, Madeline stepped up beside me. "Untie her arms and legs. I know how uncomfortable that is."

I looked down at her. "Madeline, that's a thin thread, baby. Don't push me."

She raised her eyebrows at me and leaned in toward me. "She's not going to run."

I leaned down until my face was close to hers. "Don't fucking care."

Madeline growled and then turned to look at Gina. "You want to talk. Please do it, and please make it count. Please." It sounded like Madeline was begging her to deny it to save herself.

Gina swallowed hard and nodded. She looked at Madeline for a few moments before shifting her gaze to me. I saw the fear in her eyes and the way she was trembling. I knew she had nothing to say that was going to save her. She knew it too.

"I'm sorry," she whispered.

"And that won't save you. It just confirms what Madeline won't tell me," I replied.

Madeline touched my arm then, and I tensed. I didn't want her to see the man I was about to become. The one she didn't see. The one everyone but her knew existed.

Gina's gaze went to Madeline. "I thought you were going to be temporary. That Blaise would get bored with you. That this infatuation he'd had for years … he would get it out of his system after having you." She paused and swallowed again. "But you weren't what I'd expected. I liked you, and I could see in his behavior that you were different for him. There was more there than lust. He stopped coming to check on Angel as much. He was hard to be around when you weren't with him. You had become more than a possession of his. You'd somehow possessed him." Gina let out a hard laugh. "Something no one would have thought possible."

The only reason I let her keep talking was because of the way Madeline was gripping my arm. If I stopped this, I was pretty sure she would attempt to rip it from my body. She wanted to let Gina talk, and I was going to give her that wish even if it went against every-damn-thing I was.

"He was going to move Angel back to the big house. I saw it coming before I heard him tell Garrett on the phone at the top of the stairs that he planned on moving her back. Then, he said I probably wouldn't want to go with Angel. But without Angel at his house then he wouldn't have use for me either. Why should I get to stay? He was going to want you all to himself. Without Angel, I had no role to fill for him. It's why Garrett kept me all those years ago, and I knew it. I was Angel's keeper. With her gone, I'd have to find a new place to live and I would lose the one thing I wanted most." She paused and closed her eyes tightly.

Madeline took a step closer to her, placing herself between me and Gina. She thought I didn't know what she was doing, but I did. In her pretty little head, she thought her standing there would keep Gina alive. I could easily take the shot over her head, but she knew I wouldn't do that in front of her.

"I don't have your kind of power. I knew that he'd eventually let me go when I wasn't easy access. I'd lose him, and I couldn't lose him. I'd loved him forever, and now that he saw me, I needed more time to show him that we could work. That we would be good together." She sniffled. "But you were ruining all of it. Blaise would move the guys out too. I wanted to keep the life I had here, but you were taking it all from me."

My entire body went rigid.

"Who, Gina?" Madeline asked her. The compassion clear in her tone.

Fuck me, if she said Gage, I was going to slam this damn door to keep from shooting her in the head for pure insanity.

"Levi," she whispered. "I've loved him since the first time I met him. But he never saw me. Never acted interested at all. Until six months ago. Things changed. I, uh, was with Gage, and Levi came into the room and started undressing. He joined us. He finally saw me. It had taken me years to get his attention," she said.

"And you … you bat your eyelashes at Blaise, and he is done. Ready to change it all for you."

She let out a sob, and her gaze swung to mine. "I'm sorry."

I placed a hand on Madeline's shoulder and stepped closer. "You think telling me you're fucking sorry that you took what was mine because you were fucking Levi changes anything?"

She sniffled and shook her head. "I know you won't believe me, but the guy who found me and talked me into giving them Madeline told me who he was and that her father was desperate to get to know her. That he was a good man and he'd done shit in his youth he regretted, but he wanted to know Madeline. That no harm would come to her. I believed him."

I started to step around Madeline, and she grabbed my arm and dug her nails into my skin.

"No, Blaise," she said.

Gina looked back at Madeline. "Just let him. He's right. I didn't know for sure you would be safe. The guy was attractive and charming. He seemed very sincere, but I couldn't be positive he wasn't lying. I wanted to believe him because if you were gone, then Blaise wouldn't send us all away. Let him do it. Get it over with."

"What you did isn't cause for death," Madeline said. "Besides, you tried another way to get rid of me that was safer, and it didn't work."

I looked down at her.

"You were desperate. Love can do that to you." Madeline's voice was soft and understanding.

Gina pressed her lips together, then let out another whimper before she nodded. "You weren't supposed to forgive him for killing the people you thought were your family," she said.

The rage that burned inside of me at her words made it almost impossible to keep from killing her. Knowing she'd hurt Madeline for her own benefit was unforgivable. If Madeline wasn't so fucking determined to keep Gina alive she'd be dead already. I wanted her dead.

Madeline let out a sigh. "If he hadn't told me the truth, then I probably wouldn't have."

Gina sniffled. "I like you. It was nice, having another woman around. If you hadn't been a threat to what I'd found with Levi—"

"He fucked you, Gina," I snarled. "Don't pull at her damn emotions. Levi and Gage fucked you at the same time. That isn't love. If Levi loved you, he wouldn't share you. He'd cut off Gage's dick for getting near you."

She let out a sob, as if hearing the damn truth—which she had to have already known—was hurting her. Madeline glared up at me. Had she not heard when Gina had mentioned having a threesome with Gage and Levi? She knew I was right. I'd never let another man near her.

"Wanting something so bad that you ignore reality can get you into a shitload of trouble," Huck said.

Gina bowed her head and cried harder.

Madeline took a step toward her, and I reached out to grab her arm and stop her. She looked back at my hand, then lifted her gaze to me.

"Let me go," she demanded.

"I don't want you getting in that car," I replied.

Her eyebrows drew together. "Why? Because you think she's going to lean over and bite me? She's all tied up, Blaise," Madeline said, sounding annoyed.

When this hell was over, I was taking her inside and putting her over my knee, then spanking her ass until it was bright red and she was screaming in an orgasm. I let her go and clenched my teeth to keep from saying something more.

Madeline climbed up in the backseat and pulled Gina into a hug and held her while she cried. What the fuck was wrong with my woman? She was comforting the person who had shown her photos of Luke and Cole with bullets in their heads, then lied to her and handed her over to fucking strangers. She should have taken my gun and killed Gina herself.

"How did you pause the camera system?" Huck asked her.

Gina sniffled and looked at him over Madeline's shoulder. "I don't want to answer that," she said softly.

"Why the fuck not?" I asked, stepping closer to the car.

She closed her eyes tightly. "Because you will kill someone who is innocent."

"If they showed you how to pause fucking cameras so that you could help someone abduct Madeline, then, yeah, I'm gonna fucking kill them."

Madeline turned around and looked at me with wide eyes. "But I am alive. I met my father. Nothing bad happened to me."

"But it could have," I replied. "And Gina fucking knows it."

"I don't know his name," Gina said.

"Liar," Huck drawled.

"I swear. I didn't exactly ask for it. We were at one of Mattia's parties, and Levi hadn't looked at me all night. I was going to make him jealous by flirting with this guy I didn't know. We talked, and I found out he was in security. We went to the back, and I gave him head, then told him some other things I liked to do, but first, I had a few questions for him."

She had sucked and fucked a guy to tell her how to mess with my security system. Damn slut. Levi was never going to want her. He had only been messing with her because he liked threesomes and she was willing and convenient.

"Garrett isn't going to let you live." I told her what she already knew.

Madeline was going to beg me, so my saying it was more for her sake than Gina's.

Gina nodded.

Madeline was looking at me like she wanted to punch me in the face.

"Seeing as how only the three of us have seen her," Huck said, "don't think anyone has to mention it. Madeline will take it to her damn grave. Fuck knows I don't want to see a bullet in Gina or be the sorry fucker ordered to do it."

I shifted my gaze to Huck. He shrugged. Damn asshole had known if he said this in front of Madeline, he was making it near impossible for me to do what needed to be done. I shook my head at him.

"Your call, boss," he said, although his eyes were telling me he wanted me to let him drive away and take her somewhere far from this place.

"Blaise." Madeline's pleading tone sliced through my chest. "Please. I'm safe. I got to meet my real father. We have no secrets between us now, and you know I love you completely, knowing it all. Is what she did really so bad? I think she made us stronger."

There were unshed tears in her eyes. I still had my secrets. I'd always have my fucking secrets. In my world secrets were a part of life. I would fucking lie to the Pope than tell Madeline all the shit I'd done.

"Come here," I told her.

She looked hesitant.

"Madeline," I said, then held out my hand.

She looked at my hand, then at me.

"Do you trust me?" I asked her then.

She turned back to Gina and hugged her tightly. I didn't hear what she said before she stepped out of the vehicle and walked over to take my hand.

I threaded my fingers through hers and lifted her hand to my lips and kissed it. "Let's go."

She frowned. "Go where?"

"Inside," I replied and started walking.

She kept up beside me as I pulled her along.

"What about Gina?" she asked.

I shrugged. "She ran off. We can't find her."

Madeline stopped then and pulled her hand free of mine before throwing her arms around me. "I love you," she said fiercely.

I wrapped my arms around her and held her to me, burying my face in her hair. The SUV's engine started, and I continued to hold Madeline while she lifted her head and watched it drive away over my shoulder.

Chapter THIRTY-FIVE

MADELINE

I stood inside the entrance of … our house. The ceiling was high, and there was a chandelier that hung much like the one at the Houstons'. A wide spiral staircase was to my right, and everything was bright and cheerful. It smelled like fresh paint and shone as if it was brand-new.

The past month, Blaise had brought me over here several times while they worked on the house. He'd had me choose paint colors, and we had gone shopping for furniture several times. It took a lot to fill a house this size. My favorite part had been decorating the nursery.

Knowing that our little boy would be brought home to this house after he was born made my heart swell. He would have more opportunities than I could have even dreamed up as a child, but more than that, he would know he was loved by his parents. He'd never experience a day when he was scared, or lost, or felt alone.

The fact that he would one day be a Mafia boss? I didn't want to consider that right now. That was the one thing that

I had struggled with since they had told me it was a boy. He was the heir. But first, he was my little boy.

The door opened behind me, and Blaise stepped inside, smiling at me. He was wearing his cowboy hat and jeans that hung on his hips just right. The butterflies were still there at the sight of him. I wondered if that would ever go away.

"You lose your shirt?" I asked him.

"It's hot as fuck out there," he replied.

I reached out to run my hand down his abs.

"Easy, baby, unless you want to be bent over those stairs," he warned me.

I looked up at him and smiled. "You say that like it's a threat."

He pulled me to him and covered my mouth with his. I sank into his sweaty chest and inhaled him. Even after working in the heat with horses all day, his smell still turned me on.

"I'm distracting you," I whispered. "What was it you came inside for?"

Blaise kissed me one more time, then nodded his head to the far right of the house. "Water," he said. "But this was much better."

"I'll go get it for you," I told him.

He frowned. "I can get it."

I placed a hand on my hip and smirked. "But I want to get it."

A slow, sexy grin tugged at his face. "I'll go with you."

I turned to walk through our house, taking in everything and still trying hard to believe this was where we would live. Where I would live. It was beautiful; however, I didn't require all this. I just wanted Blaise. I stopped to turn on the lights in the kitchen.

"How are you enjoying the first day in our new home?" he asked me, stepping up to grab my waist and kiss the side of my neck.

"It's just a house," I told him.

He stiffened, and I looked back at him. I knew this was something he had wanted to give me. He had needed me to have a house like this, and I'd accepted that odd compulsion he had with grace. No fighting him on it.

"Would you rather be back in the cave?" he asked me, looking concerned.

I lifted my hand and cupped the side of his face. "This is just a house, but it's not a home. You, Blaise Hughes, are my home."

Book Three Teaser...

Chapter ONE

TRINITY

Perhaps the word I was looking for was *ironic*. It seemed a harsh word and made me feel as if I were looking at this with no emotion. That couldn't be further from the truth. In the past week, I had suffered from every emotion known to man—or at least, it'd felt like it. Regardless, *ironic* was a good word. One that encompassed all that had happened in the past six months.

The soft whispers, hushed voices, even crying that I could hear on the other side of the wall I was leaning against reminded me that I should be out there. People expected me to be. They wanted to tell me how sorry they were, that they were praying for me, what a good man Hayes had been, and best of all, that it was God's plan. I, on the other hand, didn't want to endure listening to it. They knew nothing.

I wasn't sure how long I could stay in this dark prayer room until someone found me. My stepmom, Tabitha, would come looking soon enough. She wouldn't want me to embarrass her in front of the church. There had been no one more thrilled than Tabitha when Hayes proposed to me. The pastor's grandson, who would soon be a minister himself. He was loved and respected in town. He should have been. Hayes had been the most genuine, kindest, warmest, person I'd ever known. Somehow, he had chosen me.

The door opened, slamming against the wall, and I jumped, startled. My gaze shot up from the handkerchief I had been twisting in my hands, expecting to see Tabitha. My excuses were on the tip of my tongue when I froze. That was not Tabitha.

It was a man. A very large man. A slightly terrifying man. His eyes locked on me, and he watched me for a moment. I couldn't tell much in the darkness other than the silhouette of his face was defined, masculine, most likely attractive. Not that it mattered.

"You must be the missing fiancée," he said in a deep voice, letting the door close behind him.

I nodded, but said nothing.

He walked over and sat down on a bench across the room. I watched him, wanting to ask who he was and what he was doing in here. His intimidating presence, however, kept me from speaking. He had to be at least six foot four. The suit coat he was wearing seemed tight across his wide shoulders, as if it were ready to rip apart with the wrong move.

The man reached into the pocket of his coat and pulled out a flask. My eyes went wide as he opened it and took a long drink from it. When he lowered the flask, his eyes met mine again.

"You want a drink? Might help you face that out there," he said, holding it out to me.

I looked at the flask and considered it. The fact that I was even thinking about it reminded me of all that Hayes had never truly known about me.

Finally, I shook my head. "I can't have the Baptist folks smelling liquor on my breath," I said softly.

He nodded, then twisted the top back on it before putting it in his pocket. I found myself wishing there were more light in here. The only window was stained glass and small. With the dreary day outside, it didn't shine much light into the room. I was curious about what he looked like. His voice was deep, and there was a drawl to it that was oddly familiar.

"Got to fucking go out there sometime," he said, shifting his gaze from the colorful window to me.

I knew that. I was going to. As soon as I convinced myself I could survive it.

"He ever tell you about the time he shot the window out of the parsonage?" the man asked with a hint of amusement in his voice.

Was he talking about Hayes?

I shook my head.

The man smirked then, and even in the shadows, I could see the way it curled his lips. I dropped my gaze back to my lap. This was Hayes's funeral. I would not sit here and appreciate another man's good looks.

What was wrong with me? Scratch that. I knew what was wrong with me. So much that I didn't have enough time to list it all.

"He was seven. Damn, he was a strong-willed hothead back then. Thought he knew it all." The man chuckled. "Fucker didn't know shit."

I was officially intrigued. How did this man know Hayes? They weren't friends. I had met all his friends. Yet something about him made it clear he was struggling with Hayes's death as much as I was. He sighed and rubbed the back of his neck.

The door opened again, and light filled the room. This time, it was Tabitha. Her red hair was styled and sprayed so much that it wouldn't budge in a windstorm. Her frantic eyes met mine, and then there it was. The fury, the resentment—all the things she had always felt for me were once again bursting wide open. Hayes was no longer here, and she had no use for me. Except right now, and I was letting her down. I wasn't out there for all the church people to see.

"What do you think you're doing? Being a selfish brat, like you always have been. Get out there right this instant, Trinity. I will not let you embarrass this family," she spit at me with the disgust and hate in her eyes I hadn't seen since the day Hayes had walked me to my car after church and asked me out.

I started to stand up.

"She's not going anywhere until she's damn well ready to."

The deep voice startled Tabitha. She hadn't noticed the man in the darkness.

She opened the door further so that the light filled the room and shot her angry glare toward him. "Excuse me, sir," she said in her haughty voice. "You do not have a say in what she does or does not do. She will go to the sanctuary and stand there like her fiancé would have wanted her to."

The man stood up, and Tabitha had to tilt her head back to look up at him.

"She's a grown-ass woman. She can do what she wants to do. And you, lady," he said, nodding his head toward Tabitha, "don't know shit about what Hayes would have wanted."

Tabitha's eyes flared, and her lips thinned. She wasn't one to be talked down to. Even before she'd married the mayor, my father, when I was ten, she had looked down her nose at the world. Tabitha felt important, but I had no idea why.

"You don't belong here," she stated. "I have never laid eyes on you in my life, and I've known the pastor's family for over ten years. I'm going to go get Officer Randal to escort you out. You shouldn't have been in a room alone with a young girl, and language such as yours is not accepted in these walls."

I wanted to groan and cover my face. I didn't know this man, but Tabitha was embarrassing me anyway. Being connected to her was just another one of the things to add to why my life had been hell. Bad luck had struck on the day I was born when my entrance into this world killed my mom, and it had never stopped.

"Damn, I sure hope you try," the man replied with amusement in his voice rather than anger.

I lifted my gaze up to look at him now that the light was illuminating his face. Although I immediately wished I hadn't. I'd guessed he was attractive, but this wasn't something I had expected. Sure, I had noticed the defined angles of his features in the darkness, but good Lord, this man looked like sin. I swallowed hard and thought about praying for forgiveness, then remembered I wasn't praying anymore. I had given up my belief in God when I got the call that Hayes was dead.

He didn't look back at me though, and I found myself relieved. I wasn't sure I could handle seeing his eyes. Not if the rest of him looked like that.

"Trinity, now." Tabitha's voice was sharp and clearly near hysterics.

She wasn't used to being spoken to that way. I, however, would pay money for this to continue.

Hayes wouldn't want this though, and I knew it. He had wanted me to try and find peace with my stepmom. I stood up and walked over to her, not looking at the stranger, for fear I'd see disappointment in his eyes. He didn't take orders. He was his own person, and he'd just witnessed how weak I was.

Tabitha grabbed my bare arm so hard that her nails bit into my skin. I winced, but said nothing as I went with her out of the room. Perhaps if she squeezed hard enough, it would hurt so bad that I could go into the sanctuary with tears in my eyes. Because they would want me crying. They would want to see me completely broken and devastated.

What none of them understood was, I had been broken and devastated so many times in my life that it took more than the death of someone I cared deeply for to make me cry. Tears didn't come easy for me. I was twisted inside. Hayes had seen something else in me that I wanted to be. I truly wanted to be the girl he had thought I was.

Unfortunately, I never had been. There was a darkness in me that I couldn't flush out. It wouldn't go away. It called to me and made me think things. Terrible, sinful things. It was no wonder God had never once answered one of my prayers. Hayes had been the only break I'd ever gotten, and God had only allowed me to have that for six months before snatching it away too.

"You are a disgrace," Tabitha said through her teeth as she dragged me toward the entrance of the church.

I didn't argue with her because I probably was. She stopped when she saw Officer Randal and dropped her death grip on my arm.

"Officer," she said in her fake voice. The one she used here at church and in town. The one that made everyone think she was a God-fearing, church-going woman who loved the Lord. "There is a man here who doesn't belong. He went into the prayer room, where Trinity was trying to be alone to grieve. The profanity out of his mouth and disregard for the house of the Lord was awful. You need to get that man out of here. I fear he is dangerous."

It took every ounce of self-control I had not to roll my eyes. She sounded ridiculous.

"What man? Did you get a name?" Randal asked with concern in his tone.

She opened her mouth, then shut it again. Neither of us knew his name, but even if I did, I wouldn't have shared it with her. I was a fantastic liar. Her gaze swung to me, and I shrugged. Then, I saw her eyes narrow, as if she thought I was lying, but she wouldn't treat me bad in front of witnesses that mattered. The man in the prayer room did not matter to her.

"There!" She pointed, and I turned my head to see him walking down toward the sanctuary.

His dark hair was cut short, and I could see from here that his eyes were a lighter color. Not boring brown, like mine. I wasn't sure though since he wasn't looking at me. His entire body seemed to flex with each move he made. I wondered if he was one of those guys that had muscles all over. Hayes had had more of a runner's body, and he had not been built like that.

"Oh," Randal replied, and his tone dropped. "I'm, uh, sorry, Mrs. Bennett. Uh, I can't ask him to leave."

I studied Officer Randal as he shifted on his feet nervously. The large Adam's apple in his throat bobbed.

"Who is he? Surely, Pastor Darren and his family do not know this man," Tabitha said, sounding close to losing her cool.

She rarely lost a battle. If she didn't get the massive, good-looking man kicked out of the church, she'd have lost in her eyes, and that would not sit well with her.

Randal ran a hand over his slightly balding head. "He, uh, does indeed know the family," Officer Randal said. "That's Huck Kingston, Hayes's older brother."

ACKNOWLEDGMENTS

WHEW … this is a ride, y'all, and I am not getting off it anytime soon. Thankfully, there are people in my life who let me lock myself away and write the stories playing out in my head. It doesn't seem to stop with this group of characters, and in this book, you will see it just gets deeper, and the possibilities are endless.

Britt is always the first person I mention because he makes it possible for me to do this. He takes care of everything else so that I can get the story out.

Emerson, for dealing with the fact that I must write some days and she can't have my full attention. She is starting to figure out that all this typing creates actual books. Thanks to her learning to read this year, my job now makes sense to her.

My older children, who live in other states, were great about me not being able to answer their calls most of the time, and they had to wait until I could get back to them. They still love me and understand this part of Mom's world.

Beta readers, who read fast on my insane deadlines and keep up with me—Annabelle Glines, Jerilyn Martinez, and Vicci Kaighan, I love y'all!

My editor, Jovana Shirley at Unforeseen Editing, for not only doing this last minute because I suck at deadlines, but also for helping me make this story the best it could be.

My formatter, Melissa Stevens at The Illustrated Author. Her work always blows me away. It's hands down the best formatting I've ever had in my books.

Damonza, for my book cover. This cover could not be more perfect. They are always a pleasure to work with.

Abbi's Army, for being my support and cheering me on. I've had so much fun, starting this new series and reading your thoughts. I love y'all!

My readers, for allowing me to write books. Without you, this wouldn't be possible.

Made in the USA
Middletown, DE
24 September 2023

39222669R00154